HOTEL

IRIS

Yoko Ogawa

TRANSLATED FROM THE JAPANESE BY
STEPHEN SNYDER

Harvill Secker
London

Published by Harvill Secker 2010

10 9 8 7 6 5 4 3 2 1

Copyright © Yoko Ogawa 1996
English translation copyright © Stephen Snyder 2010
English translation rights arranged with Yoko Ogawa
through Japan Foreign-Rights Centre / Anna Stein

Yoko Ogawa has asserted her right under the Copyright,
Designs and Patents Act 1988 to be identified as the author of this work

First published with the title *Hotel Iris* in 1996 by Gakken, Tokyo

First published in Great Britain in 2010 by
Harvill Secker
Random House
20 Vauxhall Bridge Road
London SW1V 2SA

www.rbooks.co.uk

Addresses for companies within The Random House Group Limited can be found at:
www.randomhouse.co.uk/offices.htm

The Random House Group Limited Reg. No. 954009

A CIP catalogue record for this book is available from the British Library

ISBN 9781846554032

The Random House Group Limited supports The Forest Stewardship
Council (FSC), the leading international forest certification organisation. All our titles
that are printed on Greenpeace approved FSC certified paper carry the FSC logo.
Our paper procurement policy can be found at
www.rbooks.co.uk/environment

Mixed Sources
Product group from well-managed
forests and other controlled sources
www.fsc.org Cert no. TT-COC-2139
© 1996 Forest Stewardship Council
FSC

Printed and bound in Great Britain by
CPI Mackays, Chatham, ME5 8TD

HOTEL IRIS

He first came to the Iris one day just before the beginning of the summer season. The rain had been falling since dawn. It grew heavier at dusk, and the sea was rough and gray. A gust blew open the door, and rain soaked the carpet in the lobby. The shopkeepers in the neighborhood had turned off their neon signs along the empty streets. A car passed from time to time, its headlights shining through the raindrops.

I was about to lock up the cash register and turn out the lights in the lobby, when I heard something heavy hitting the floor above, followed by a woman's scream. It was a very long scream—so long that I started to wonder before it ended whether she wasn't laughing instead.

"Filthy pervert!" The scream stopped at last, and a woman came flying out of Room 202. "You disgusting old man!" She caught her foot on a seam in the carpet and fell on the landing, but she went on hurling insults at the door of the room. "What do you think I am? You're not fit to be with a woman like me! Scumbag! Impotent bastard!"

She was obviously a prostitute—even I could tell that much—and no longer young. Frizzy hair hung at her wrinkled neck, and thick, shiny lipstick had smeared onto her cheeks. Her mascara had run, and her left breast hung out of her blouse where the buttons had come undone. Pale pink thighs protruded from a short skirt, marked in places with red scratches. She had lost one of her cheap plastic high heels.

Her insults stopped for a moment, but then a pillow flew out of the room, hitting her square in the face, and the screaming started all over again. The pillow lay on the landing, smeared with lipstick. Roused by the noise, a few guests had now gathered in the hall in their pajamas. My mother appeared from our apartment in the back.

"You pervert! Creep! You're not fit for a cat in heat." The prostitute's voice, ragged and hoarse with tears, dissolved into coughs and sobs as one object after another came flying out of the room: a hanger, a crumpled bra, the missing high heel, a handbag. The handbag fell open, and the contents scattered across the hall. The woman clearly wanted to escape down the stairs, but she was too flustered to get to her feet—or perhaps she had turned an ankle.

"Shut up! We're trying to sleep!" one of the guests shouted from down the hall, and the others started complaining all at once. Only Room 202 was perfectly silent. I couldn't see the occupant, and he hadn't said a word. The only signs of his

existence were the woman's horrible glare and the objects flying out at her.

"I'm sorry," my mother interrupted, coming to the bottom
of the stairs, "but I'm afraid I'm going to have to ask you to
leave."

"You don't have to tell me!" the woman shouted. "I'm going!"

"I'll be calling the police, of course," Mother said, to no
one in particular. "But please," she added, turning to the other
guests, "don't think anything more about it. Good night. I'm
sorry you've been disturbed. . . . And as for you," she went on,
calling up to the man in Room 202, "you're going to have
to pay for all of this, and I don't mean just the price of the
room." On her way to the second floor, Mother passed the
woman. She had scraped the contents back into the bag and
was stumbling down the stairs without even bothering to
button her blouse. One of the guests whistled at her exposed
breast.

"Just a minute, you," Mother said into the darkened room
and to the prostitute on the stairs. "Who's going to pay? You
can't just slip out after all this fuss." Mother's first concern
was always the money. The prostitute ignored her, but at that
moment a voice rang out from above.

"Shut up, whore." The voice seemed to pass through us,
silencing the whole hotel. It was powerful and deep, but with
no trace of anger. Instead, it was almost serene, like a hypnotic
note from a cello or a horn.

I turned to find the man standing on the landing. He was

past middle age, on the verge of being old. He wore a pressed white shirt and dark brown pants, and he held a jacket of the same material in his hand. Though the woman was completely disheveled, he was not even breathing heavily. Nor did he seem particularly embarrassed. Only the few tangled hairs on his forehead suggested that anything was out of the ordinary.

It occurred to me that I had never heard such a beautiful voice giving an order. It was calm and imposing, with no hint of indecision. Even the word "whore" was somehow appealing.

"Shut up, whore." I tried repeating it to myself, hoping I might hear him say the word again. But he said nothing more.

The woman turned and spat at him pathetically before walking out the door. The spray of saliva fell on the carpet.

"You'll have to pay for everything," Mother said, rounding on the man once more. "The cleaning, and something extra for the trouble you've caused. And you are not welcome here again, understand? I don't take customers who make trouble with women. Don't you forget it."

The other guests went slowly back to their rooms. The man slipped on his jacket and walked down the stairs in silence, never raising his eyes. He pulled two bills from his pocket and tossed them on the counter. They lay there for a moment, crumpled pathetically, before I took them and smoothed them carefully on my palm. They were slightly warm from the man's body. He walked out into the rain without so much as a glance in my direction.

I've always wondered how our inn came to be called the Hotel Iris. All the other hotels in the area have names that have to do with the sea.

"It's a beautiful flower, and the name of the rainbow goddess in Greek mythology. Pretty stylish, don't you think?" When I was a child, my grandfather had offered this explanation.

Still, there were no irises blooming in the courtyard, no roses or pansies or daffodils either. Just an overgrown dogwood, a zelkova tree, and some weeds. There was a small fountain made of bricks, but it hadn't worked in a long time. In the middle of the fountain stood a plaster statue of a curly-haired boy in a long coat. His head was cocked to one side and he was playing the harp, but his face had no lips or eyelids and was covered with bird droppings. I wondered where my grandfather had come up with the story about the goddess, since no one in our family knew anything about literature, let alone Greek mythology.

I tried to imagine the goddess—slender neck, full breasts, eyes staring off into the distance. And a robe with all the colors of the rainbow. One shake of that robe could cast a spell of beauty over the whole earth. I always thought that if the goddess of the rainbow would come to our hotel for even a few minutes, the boy in the fountain would learn to play happy tunes on his harp.

The R in IRIS on the sign on the roof had come loose and was tilted a bit to the right. It looked a little silly, but also slightly sinister. In any event, no one ever thought to fix it.

Our family lived in the three dark rooms behind the front desk. When I was born, there were five of us. My grandmother was the first to go, but that was while I was still a baby so I don't remember it. She died of a bad heart, I think. Next was my father. I was eight then, so I remember everything.

And then it was grandfather's turn. He died two years ago. He got cancer in his pancreas or his gallbladder—somewhere in his stomach—and it spread to his bones and his lungs and his brain. He suffered for almost six months, but he died in his own bed. We had given him one of the good mattresses, from a guest room, but only after it had broken a spring. Whenever he turned over in bed, it sounded like someone stepping on a frog.

My job was to sterilize the tube that came out of his right side and to empty the fluid that had collected in the bag at the end of it. Mother made me do this every day after school, though I was afraid to touch the tube. If you didn't do it right, the tube fell out of his side, and I always imagined that his organs were going to spurt from the hole it left. The liquid in the bag was a beautiful shade of yellow, and I often wondered why something so pretty was hidden away inside the body. I emptied it into the fountain in the courtyard, wetting the toes of the harp-playing boy.

Grandfather suffered all the time, but the hour just before dawn was especially bad. His groans echoed in the dark, mingling with the croaking of the mattress. We kept the shutters closed, but the guests still complained about the noise.

"I'm terribly sorry," Mother would tell them, her voice sickly sweet, her pen tapping nervously on the counter. "All those cats seem to be in heat at the same time."

We kept the hotel open even on the day grandfather died. It was off-season and we should have been nearly empty, but for some reason a women's choir had booked several rooms. Strains of "Edelweiss" or "When It's Lamp-Lighting Time in the Valley" or "Lorelei" filled the pauses in the funeral prayers. The priest pretended not to hear and went on with the service, eyes fixed on the floor in front of him. The woman who owned the dress shop—an old drinking friend of Grandfather's—sobbed at one point as a soprano in the choir hit a high note and together it sounded almost like harmony. The ladies were singing in every corner of the hotel—in the bath, in the dining room, out on the veranda—and their voices fell like a shroud over Grandfather's body. But the goddess of the rainbow never came to shake her robe for him.

I saw the man from Room 202 again two weeks later. It was Sunday, and I was out doing some errands for Mother. The sky was clear and the day so warm I'd begun to sweat. Some kids were on the beach trying to get the first tan of the year.

The tide was out, and the rocks along the coast were exposed all the way to the seawall. Though it was early in the season, a few tourists could be seen on the restaurant terraces and the excursion boat dock. The sea was still chilly, but the sunlight on the seawall and the bustle in town made it clear that summer was not far off.

Our town came to life for just three months each year. It huddled, silent as a stone, from fall through spring. But then it would suddenly yield to the sea's gentle embrace. The sun shone on the golden beach. The crumbling seawall was exposed at low tide, and hills rising from beyond the cape turned green. The streets were filled with people enjoying their holidays. Parasols opened, fountains frothed, champagne corks popped, and fireworks lit up the night sky. The restaurants, bars, hotels, and excursion boats, the souvenir shops, the marinas—and even our Iris—were dressed up for summer. Though in the case of the Iris, this meant little more than rolling down the awnings on the terrace, turning up the lights in the lobby, and putting out the sign with the high-season rates.

Then, a few months later, the summer would end just as suddenly as it had begun. The wind shifted, the pattern of the waves changed, and all the people returned to places that are completely unknown to me. The discarded foil from an ice cream cone that yesterday had glittered festively by the side of the road overnight would become no more than a piece of trash. But that was three months away; and so, without a care, I went out to do Mother's shopping.

I recognized the man immediately. He was buying tooth-paste at the housewares shop. I hadn't looked at him care-fully that night at the Iris, but there was something familiar about the shape of his body and his hands as he stood under the pale fluorescent light. Next, he seemed to be choosing laundry detergent. He took a long time with the decision, picking up each box, studying the label, and then checking the price. He put a box in his basket, but then he read the label again and returned it to the shelf. His attention seemed completely focused on the soap; in the end, he chose the cheapest brand.

I cannot explain why I decided to follow him that day. I didn't feel particularly curious about what had happened at the Iris, but those words, his command, had stayed with me.

After leaving the shop, he went to the pharmacy. He handed over what appeared to be a prescription and was given two packets of medicine. Tucking these into his coat pocket, he walked on to the stationer's, two doors down the street. I leaned against the lamppost and cautiously looked inside. He had apparently brought a fountain pen to be re-paired, and there was a long exchange with the shopkeeper. The man dismantled the pen and pointed at one piece after the other, complaining about something. The owner of the store was clearly upset, too, but the man ignored him and went on with his complaints. It occurred to me how much I wanted to hear his voice. Finally, the shopkeeper seemed to agree reluctantly to his demands.

Next, he walked east on the shore road. He wore a suit,

and his tie was neatly knotted, despite the heat. He held himself stiffly and looked straight ahead as he walked, keeping a good pace. The plastic bag containing the laundry detergent dangled at his side, and the packets of medicine made a bulge in his coat pocket. The street was crowded, and from time to time his bag bumped a passerby, but no one noticed or turned to look back. I was the only one who seemed to see him, and that made me all the more intent on my strange little game.

A boy about my age was playing the accordion in front of the giant clock made of flowers in the plaza; perhaps because the instrument was old, or because of the way he played it, the song sounded sad and thin.

The man stopped and listened for a moment, though no one else seemed interested in the boy's performance. I watched from a short way off. In the background, the hands of the clock turned slowly around the floral face.

The man threw a coin in the accordion case. It made a soft thud. The boy bowed, but the man turned and walked off. Something about the boy's face reminded me of the statue in our courtyard.

How far was I going to follow him? The only thing that I'd bought on Mother's list was the toothpaste. I began to worry. Mother would be angry that I was still out when the guests started arriving, but I couldn't take my eyes off the man's back.

He reached the excursion boat dock and stepped into the waiting room. Was he planning to take a ride? The room was crowded with families and young couples. Several times a day, the boat sailed out to an island about a half hour away from the shore, briefly docking at the wharf before returning to the mainland. The next boat wouldn't be leaving for twenty-five minutes.

"Young lady. Why are you following me?" At first, I didn't realize he was speaking to me—the room was so noisy and the words so unexpected—but finally I recognized the voice that had shouted at the Iris. "Is there something I can do for you?"

I shook my head quickly, startled to have been caught, but the man seemed even more frightened than I was. He blinked nervously and ran his tongue over his lips. I found it difficult to believe that this was the same man who had uttered that magnificent command at the Iris that night.

"You're the girl from the hotel, aren't you?"

"Yes," I said, not daring to look directly at him.

"You were sitting at the front desk that night. I recognized you right away."

A group of elementary school children filed into the waiting room, pushing us back against the windows. I wondered uneasily what the man intended to do with me. I'd never planned to speak to him, but now I didn't know how to get away.

"Did you have something you wanted to say? Perhaps you were going to scold me?"

"Oh no! Not at all . . ."

"Still, I apologize for the other day. It must have been unpleasant for you." His tone was polite, quite unlike the

man who had shouted in the lobby of the Iris, and this somehow made me even more nervous.

"Please don't worry about what my mother said. You were
very generous when you paid the bill."

"But it was a terrible night."

"That awful rain . . ."

"Yes, but I mean I'm still not sure how things ended up
the way they did. . . ."

I remembered that I had found a bra wadded up on the
landing after they left that night. It was lavender, with gaudy
lace, and I had gathered it up like the carcass of a dead ani-
mal and tossed it in the trash bin in the kitchen.

The children were running wildly around the waiting
room. The sun was still high in the sky, sparkling on the sea
outside the window. The island in the distance, as everyone
in town seemed to agree, was shaped like a human ear. The
excursion boat had just rounded the lobe of the island and
was heading back toward us. A gull rested on each post of
the pier.

Now that I was standing next to him, the man seemed
smaller than I had imagined. He was about my height, but
his chest and shoulders were thin and frail. His hair was even
more neatly combed now, but I could see a bald spot in back.

We stood quietly for a moment, looking out at the sea.
There was nothing else to do. The man grimaced in the
bright sunlight, as though he'd felt a sudden pain.

"Are you taking the boat?" I asked at last, suffocated by
the silence.

"I am," he said.

"People who live here don't usually ride it. I did it only once, when I was little."

"But I live on the island."

"I didn't know anyone actually lived there."

"There are a few of us. This is how we get home." There was a diving shop on the island and a sanatarium for employees of a steel company, but I hadn't known about any houses. The man rolled and twisted his tie as he spoke, creasing the tip. The boat was getting closer, and the children had begun lining up impatiently by the gate. "The other passengers have cameras or fishing poles or snorkels—I'm the only one with a shopping bag."

"But why would you want to live in such an inconvenient place?"

"I'm comfortable there, and I work at home."

"What kind of work?"

"I'm a translator—from Russian."

"Translator . . . ," I repeated slowly to myself.

"Does that seem odd?"

"No, it's just that I've never met a translator before."

"It's a simple sort of job, really. You sit at a desk all day long, looking up words in a dictionary. And you? Are you in high school?"

"No, I tried it for a few months, but I dropped out."

"I see. And how old are you?"

"Seventeen."

"Seventeen . . . ," he repeated, savoring each syllable.

"There's something wonderful about taking a boat to get home," I said.

"I have a small place. It was built a long time ago, a cottage on the far side from where the boat docks. Just about here on the ear," he said, tilting his head toward me and pointing at his own earlobe. As I bent forward to look at the spot, our bodies nearly touched for a moment. He pulled back immediately, and I looked away. That was the first time I realized that the shape of an ear changes with age. His was no more than a limp sliver of dark flesh.

The excursion boat blew its horn as it pulled up to the dock, scattering the gulls in a cloud. The loudspeaker in the waiting room announced the departure, and someone unhooked the chain at the entrance.

"I have to be going," the translator muttered.

"Good-bye," I said.

"Good-bye." I felt as though we were saying something far more important than a simple farewell.

I could see him from the window as he joined the line of passengers and made his way along the pier. He was short, but there was no mistaking his suit in the crowd of tourists. Suddenly, he turned to look back and I waved to him, though it seemed absurd to be waving to a stranger whose name I didn't even know. I thought he was about to wave back, but then he thrust his hand in his pocket, as if embarrassed.

The boat blew its horn and pulled away from the dock.

———

Mother was furious when I got home. It was past five o'clock, and I had forgotten to pick up her dress at the dry cleaner's.

"How could you forget?" she said. "You knew I was planning to wear it to the exhibition tonight." Someone was ringing the bell at the front desk. "It's the only dancing dress I have, and I can't go without it. You know that. The exhibition starts at five thirty. I'll never make it now. I've been waiting all this time. You've spoiled everything."

"I'm sorry, Mama. I met an old woman in town who was feeling ill. She was pale and shaking all over, so I took her to the clinic. I couldn't just leave her there. . . . That's why I'm late." This was the lie I'd come up with on my way home. The bell rang again, enraging Mother.

"Go get it!" she screamed.

The "exhibition" was nothing more than a humdrum little function where shopkeepers' wives, cannery workers, and a few retirees could dance. It was a miserable thing, really, and if I had remembered the dress, she would probably have decided that it wasn't worth the trouble to go.

I have never seen my mother dance. But it makes me a little queasy to imagine her calves shaking, her feet spilling out of her shoes, her makeup running with sweat, a strange man's hand at her waist. . . .

Since I was a little girl, Mother has praised my appearance to anyone who would listen. Her favorite customers are the big tippers, but the ones who tell her I'm beautiful run a close second, even when they aren't particularly sincere.

"Have you ever seen such transparent skin? It's almost

scary the way you can see right through it. She has the same big, dark eyes and long lashes she did when she was a baby. When I took her out, people were constantly stopping me to tell me how cute she was. And there was even a sculptor who made a statue of her—it won first prize in some show." Mother has a thousand ways to brag about my looks, but half of them are lies. The sculptor was a pedophile who nearly raped me.

If Mother is so intent on paying me compliments, it might be because she doesn't really love me very much. In fact, the more she tells me how pretty I am, the uglier I feel. To be honest, I have never once thought of myself as pretty.

She still does my hair every morning. She sits me down at the dressing table and takes hold of my ponytail, forcing me to keep very still. When she starts in with the brush, I can barely stand it, but if I move my head even the least bit, she tightens her grip.

She combs in camellia oil, making sure every hair is lacquered in place. I hate the smell. Sometimes she pins it up with a cheap barrette.

"There," she says, with deep satisfaction in her voice, "all done." I feel as though she's hurt me in a way that will never heal.

I was sent to bed without any dinner that night—the usual punishment since I was little. Nights when my stomach is empty have always seemed darker, but as I lay there I found myself tracing the shape of the man's back and ear over and over in my mind.

Mother took extra care with my hair the next morning, using more oil than usual. And she made an even bigger fuss about how pretty I am.

The Iris came into being when my great-grandfather fixed up an old inn and turned it into a hotel. That was more than a hundred years ago. In that part of town, a restaurant or hotel was either supposed to have an ocean view or to be right on the beach. The Iris didn't qualify on either count: it took more than half an hour to walk to the sea, and only two of the rooms had views. The rest looked out over the fish-processing factory.

After Grandfather died, Mother made me quit school to help at the hotel. My day begins in the kitchen, getting ready for breakfast. I wash fruit, cut up ham and cheese, and arrange tubs of yogurt in a bowl of ice. As soon as I hear the first guests coming down, I grind the coffee beans and warm the bread. Then, at checkout time, I total the bills. I do all of this while saying as little as possible. Some of the guests try to make small talk, but I just smile back. I find it painful to speak to people I don't know, and besides, Mother scolds me if I make a mistake with the cash register and the receipts are off.

The woman who works for us as a maid comes just before noon, and she and Mother begin cleaning the guest rooms. In the meantime, I straighten the kitchen and the dining room. I also answer the phone to take reservations, or to talk to the linen company or the tourist board. When Mother finishes the cleaning, she comes to check on me. If she finds even one hair out of place, she immediately combs it down. Then we get ready to welcome the new guests.

Most of my day is spent at the front desk. The space behind the desk is so small and cramped you can reach just about anything you need without moving—the bell, the old-fashioned cash register, the guest book, the pen, the phone, the tourist pamphlets. The counter itself is scarred and dark from all the hands that have touched it.

As I sit slumped behind the desk, the smell of raw fish drifts in from the factory across the way, and I can see the steam from the machines that make fish paste seeping through gaps in the factory windows. Stray cats are always gathered under the delivery trucks, waiting for something to spill from the flatbeds.

My senses seem sharpest when the guests are all checked in, settled in their rooms getting ready for bed. From my stool behind the desk, I can hear and smell and feel everything happening in the hotel. I can't say I have much experience or even any real desires of my own, but just by shutting myself up behind the desk, I can imagine every scene being played out by the people spending the night at the Iris. Then I erase them one by one and find a quiet place to lie down and sleep.

———

A letter from the translator arrived on Friday morning. The handwriting was very beautiful. Taking refuge in the corner behind the desk, I read it as discreetly as I could.

My Dear Mari,

Please forgive me for writing to you like this, but it was such a great and unexpected pleasure to speak with you on Sunday afternoon in the waiting room at the dock. At my age, few things are unexpected, and one spends considerable effort avoiding shocks and disappointments. I don't suppose you would understand, but it is the sort of mental habit you develop when you reach old age.

But this past Sunday was different. Time seemed to have stopped, and I found myself being led to a place I had never even imagined.

It would be only natural that you despise me for the disgusting incident I provoked at the hotel, and I had been hoping even before we met to make a proper apology. But the open and completely unguarded way you looked at me left me so bewildered that I was unable to say anything to the point. Thus, I wish to offer you my apologies in this letter.

I have lived alone for a long time now, and I spend my days locked away on the island with my translations. I have very few friends, and I have never known a beautiful girl like you. It has been decades since anyone waved good-bye to me the way you did. I have walked along that dock countless times, but always alone, never once having cause to turn back to look for anyone.

You waved to me as if I were an old friend, and that gesture—insignificant to you—was enormously important to me. I want to thank you . . . and thank you again.

I come into town every Sunday to do my shopping, and I will be in front of the flower clock in the plaza about two o'clock in the afternoon. I wonder whether I shall have the good fortune to see you there again. I have no intention of trying to extract a promise from you—think of my request as simply an old man's ramblings. Don't give it a second thought.

The days seem to grow steadily warmer, and I suspect you will be busier at the hotel. Please take care of yourself.

P.S. I know it was rude of me, but I took the liberty of finding out your name. By coincidence, the heroine of the novel I am translating now is named Marie.

"How good of you to come," he said as soon as he saw me.

"No, not at all," I said.

Then he stared at his feet, seeming more confused than pleased. He fiddled nervously with the end of his necktie, searching for something else to say.

We stood for a while, listening to the accordion. The boy was playing, just as he had last week. I don't know whether the songs were the same, but they had the same low, ragged sound. Only a few coins had been tossed into his case. The long hand of the flower clock pointed to the five, which was made out of salvias.

"Shall we walk a bit?" said the translator, taking a coin from his pocket. He dropped it with a clatter in the case as we set off.

The shore road was in the full bloom of summer. The bars

and restaurants had opened their terraces, ice cream stands had sprung up here and there, and the workmen had begun assembling the bathhouses on the beach. The sea was covered with boats, the sunlight glittering on their sails. And yet all the brilliance of the season did not touch the translator. He wore his usual dark suit and plain tie. His clothes were neat and tidy but somehow tired.

We walked away from the dock, wandering along the road.

"Is the hotel full today?"

"No, we have just three rooms booked. That's disappointing for a Sunday, but it's because the high tide will be covering up the seawall. . . ."

"I suppose that's right."

"How long have you lived on the island?"

"More than twenty years now."

"Always by yourself?"

"Yes . . ."

We spoke little to one another, but I was acutely conscious of the translator's body next to me. Out of the corner of my eye, I followed his smallest movements—swerving to avoid a lamppost, brushing a thread from his suit, or coughing quietly as he looked down at the pavement.

I suppose I was watching him so carefully because I had never really walked next to anyone before. My father had died while I was quite young, and my mother always walked ahead of me. I'd never had a boyfriend, or even girlfriends, to walk with in town. I was confused and a bit embarrassed to have another body next to mine.

"I doubted you'd come," he said. We had reached the end of the cape and sat down on a bench.

"Why?"

"Why would a seventeen-year-old girl want to spend her Sunday with an old man like me?"

"But if I stayed home, I would just have to work. And who wouldn't want to go for a walk with someone who's so pleased by a little wave good-bye?"

The truth was I couldn't bear to think about the translator standing there at the flower clock all by himself. If I had ignored his letter and sat behind the front desk as two o'clock passed, I wouldn't have been able to think of anything else. I had seen him left standing alone at the Iris, exposed to the curious stares of the other guests, and I didn't want that scene repeated in the park on my account.

"The Marie in your Russian novel," I said. "What's she like?"

"She's a beautiful and intelligent woman. She rides well and makes intricate lace. Somewhere in the novel it says that she is 'as lovely as a flower petal touched by the morning dew.'"

"Then only our names are similar."

"This Marie falls in love with her riding master, and their love is the most sublime and intense in all the world."

"She sounds less and less like me."

"The moment I saw you at the hotel, I thought of that other Marie. You were so much like how I see her, as I'm translating the novel. You can only imagine how shocked I was when I learned that your name is Mari."

"My father gave me that name."

"It's lovely. And it suits you perfectly." He crossed his legs and squinted out at the sea. I felt as though my father had paid me a compliment.

Few tourists came out to the end of the cape, and the benches nearby were empty. The wildflowers blooming on the hillside arched in the breeze. A fenced path led up the hill behind us, offering views of the sea all the way to the top.

The shore road stretched on into the distance. The high tide lapped at the seawall, and the translator's island was dimly visible in the distance.

"I've never read a Russian novel," I said.

"When my translation is finished, you'll be the first to see it."

"But I won't understand it."

"I'm sure you will. It's straightforward enough."

"Could I find other books you've translated at the library?"

"No, I'm afraid not. You see, I'm not a real translator, the sort a publisher would commission to do a novel." I had never thought about what it meant to be a "real" translator, but he seemed so sad as he made this confession. "I translate guidebooks and commercial pamphlets and a column for a magazine. Sometimes I do advertisements for medicines, manuals for electronic devices, business correspondence, even Russian recipes. It's quite dull. As for Marie's novel, no one asked me to translate it—it's for my own amusement."

"But I think it's wonderful—helping people understand things they could never know otherwise!"

"No one has ever put it that way."

The awkwardness between us had begun to ebb, and from time to time I glanced over at him as I asked him questions. He had stopped fidgeting with his tie, but he remained as timid as ever. I thought at first that he was still embarrassed by what had happened that night at the hotel, but it slowly dawned on me that he was simply afraid an errant word or look would cause the girl sitting next to him to dissolve into thin air. It seemed strange to me that he could be so fearful at his age.

He brushed a blade of grass from the bench. When he noticed a cabbage moth hovering around the flowers at his feet, he pulled back his legs to avoid disturbing it. There were age spots on his hands, and the knot of his tie sunk into the wrinkles on his neck. His face was ordinary, but his ears were remarkable.

"Do you have a family?" I asked.

"No," he said. It was, in fact, difficult to imagine the kind of family that had raised him, what kind of parents he'd had, or even the house where he lived on the island. He seemed to exist outside of time, as though he had just appeared from nowhere on the landing at the Iris. "I was married once, when

I was thirty-five, but my wife died three years later. After that I moved to the island."

The sky brightened and it grew warm. A couple strolled by—little more than footsteps in gravel, close and then far away. I wondered what we looked like to them. A grandfather and his granddaughter? A teacher and his pupil? Or could they see that there was no link of any kind between us?

A steady breeze blew off the water, and I had to pat down my skirt from time to time. Whitecaps flecked the waves.

"If you're warm, you should take off your jacket," I said.

"No, I'm fine like this."

We stared out at the sea in silence, more at ease with each other than before—as if the silence had become a soft veil covering the two of us.

The waves crashed at our feet. Shorebirds cried out in the distance. Beneath the veil, the sounds were wonderfully clear and distinct, even the quiet rasping of the translator's breath.

"I suppose I should be getting back," I said at last.

"Thank you for coming today," he said.

The waiting room at the dock was less crowded, perhaps because it was later in the day. The loudspeaker urged passengers to board.

"Would you be so kind as to wave again today?"

"Of course."

A faint smile brightened his eyes for a moment and then faded.

"Thank you," he said again, reaching out to touch my cheek with the tips of his fingers. My breath caught in my throat and I stiffened. The feeling was not unpleasant—his gesture had been a natural expression of gratitude—but my heart was beating so hard it was almost painful. I looked down, unsure how to respond. His fingers passed lightly over my ear and lingered in my hair.

"Lovely," he said. I realized he was trembling, though it was only my hair he was touching. I stared at the floor, unable to move, worrying that my hair still smelled of camellia oil. What if he disliked it as much as I did?

The rays of the setting sun fell across the pier. I waved from the window of the waiting room, just as I'd promised. It no longer seemed ridiculous—in fact, I felt it was the most important thing I could be doing at that moment.

He turned at the bottom of the stairs. The sunlight was too bright for me to see his face clearly, but he must have spotted me in the window since he raised his hand to wave. When the ship sailed, I put my hand to the spot where he had touched my hair. It was still neatly combed into place from the morning.

"Yes, she was very nice to me. She served tea and lots of sweets . . . cream puffs and fruitcake and sherbet . . . all kinds of imported things I'd never seen before. She's kind and very elegant. She lives in a fancy apartment on the other side of the square, with five big rooms all to herself. She thanked me over and over . . . even though all I did was help her get to the clinic. She must be very lonely. She brought out her old albums and showed me her collection of drawings, played records—anything to entertain me. I told her I had to get home, but she kept finding something else to show me . . . which is why I'm so late. I'm sorry, Mother."

The lies came to me much more easily than I would have imagined, and I felt no guilt at all. On the contrary, it was almost amusing to watch the first lie give birth to all the others. As I talked on and on about imaginary sweets and apartments, I was thinking about the translator—the wrinkles in his tie, the cabbage moth at his feet.

"Is that so?" My mother seemed only vaguely interested. "But she didn't send anything home with you? She isn't a very thoughtful old lady, is she?"

"I ate so much while I was there," I said, afraid she might be suspicious. "I couldn't have eaten anything more. I'm so full I don't need dinner tonight."

I was anxious to be alone, to hide behind the front desk and think over everything that had happened today. I was worried it would fade into shadows if I didn't.

Very soon, I began waiting for the mailman, who arrived each morning at 11:00. The translator had come up with a name that seemed suitable for a wealthy old woman, and if Mother intercepted a letter, I was prepared to say that I was corresponding with my new friend. Fortunately, she was always elsewhere when the mail arrived.

The mailman was a nice young man who brought the letters and packages all the way to the front desk, and he usually had something to say about the weather or business at the hotel. I just nodded in answer.

Once his bicycle had disappeared down the street, I would wait awhile before reaching for the packet of mail he'd left on the counter. It seemed a shame to end the pleasure of anticipation too quickly—or perhaps I was afraid there would be no letter that day.

I realized that I had waited like this in the past for my father to come home. Each night I prayed that he would be sober, and I lay awake in bed, listening for the smallest noise. My nighttime job was waiting, but I usually fell asleep, exhausted. In the morning, I would wake to the sound of my parents arguing, and the knowledge that my prayers hadn't been answered.

Then one night my father didn't come home at all. He was still missing the next day, and my mother scolded me for running out of the lobby again and again to see if he was coming down the street. His body was found late that night, his face so swollen and covered in blood that it was almost unrecognizable. After that, I stopped waiting.

There was nothing of great importance in the translator's letters—the arrival of summer, his work, the progress of Marie's romance, references to our walk on the cape—but I enjoyed his formal, slightly peculiar way of expressing himself.

The most important minutes of my day were those spent hidden behind the front desk, poring over his letters. I would cut open the envelope with great care, read the letter three or four times, and then refold it exactly along the creases he had made.

I found it hard to remember his face. There was nothing to distinguish it in my mind except the shadow of age. What I did recall was his downcast look, the way he laced his fingers from time to time, his breathing, certain tones of voice. I could summon up these separate features, but when I tried to bring them together, everything became vague and confused.

In the early afternoon, when Mother was at her dance lesson and the arrival of the guests was still hours away, I would take his letters from my pocket and with my finger follow the blue-black characters, from the greeting—"My Dear Mari"—through to the very end. I could feel the words staring back at me from the page, a sensation strangely similar to the feeling of his fingers in my hair, of him seeking me, demanding something of me.

"Have some more, Mari. Here, give me your plate."

An old friend of my mother's came to help with the cleaning. Her husband had died some years earlier, and she made ends meet by working as a dressmaker and as a part-time maid at the Iris. She ate lunch with us every day, and Mother complained behind her back that she ate too much. But Mother tolerated her because she worked hard.

"Young people have to eat," she said, offering me more potato salad. "It's the most important thing." Then she scooped some onto her own plate as well.

She and my mother chatted as they ate their lunch, gossiping about mutual acquaintances, and they drank two glasses of wine each. If the telephone at the front desk rang or a delivery truck showed up at the kitchen door, it was my job to get up and take care of it.

"Mari, do you have a boyfriend?" From time to time the maid would ask me something like this, but I would simply shrug it off. "It can't be much fun being cooped up in the hotel all the time. You should fix yourself up a bit and get out. Even a pretty girl like you has to make a bit of an effort or the boys will never notice. I'll sew a dress for you one day soon, tight through the hips but with a little flounce in the bodice, something sexy. Would you like that?" She took a sip of wine, giggling to herself. She had never once sewn anything for me.

I had discovered that she was a bit of a kleptomaniac, though she seemed to limit her thefts to things of little or no value. What's more, she never took hotel property or anything else Mother might have noticed.

The first thing that disappeared was my compass. I had used it for math class but then stuffed it away in the back of a drawer. I noticed one day that it was gone, but since I didn't need it, I hardly bothered to look for it.

Next was a butter knife from the kitchen, then a rusty old razor from the sink, some gauze from the medicine cabinet.

When my small beaded purse disappeared, I realized that something was wrong. One of my handkerchiefs, some buttons, stockings, a petticoat, all gone. But the things Mother used for my hair—combs, pins, camellia oil—these never went missing, perhaps because the maid knew how important they were to Mother.

One day I noticed the beaded purse, the one I had bought at a temple fair when I was small, peeking out of her bag. She had stuffed it with a lipstick, change, receipts. I said nothing. I was actually more worried that Mother would notice my purse in her friend's bag than I was about catching the thief, so at the first opportunity I discreetly closed the bag. But little items continued to vanish one by one from my world.

"Mari is still a child," Mother said, lighting a cigarette.

"By the way," said the woman, reaching for a piece of fried fish Mother had left on the plate, "a customer who came in to have a coat hemmed mentioned that man who made a fuss with the prostitute." My fork froze in the potato salad. "It seems that wasn't the first time he'd done something like that."

"I'm not surprised," Mother said. "That kind never learns. I'm sure he wanted that woman to do all sorts of disgusting things."

"What kinds of things?"

"Now how would I know?" Mother laughed and drained the rest of her wine. I looked down at my plate, poking at the food with my fork.

"They say he's very odd. No one knows what he does for a living, but he wanders around in a suit, even when it's sweltering."

"Like all perverts."

"My customer said she saw him at the supermarket one day, complaining that the bread he'd bought was moldy. He was putting on airs and being terribly rude—though apparently he's usually quite timid—and he had this awful look on his face, as though it were a matter of life and death. He was shaking his fist, and he even made the young woman at the store cry—all over a loaf of bread."

"He was hateful here, why should he be any different there?"

"And did you know that he lives out on the island?"

"A regular lunatic."

"There's even a rumor he's hiding here because he killed his wife."

"A murderer? Really? That's all we need!" Mother blew cigarette smoke above the dirty dishes as her friend licked grease from her fingers.

I churned my fork in the potato salad, less upset by the idea that the translator might be a murderer than by the fact that they felt free to talk this way about him. I stuffed some salad in my mouth and tried to swallow, but the potatoes caught in my throat.

The most memorable guest we've had at the hotel was a foreign woman named Iris. A fax in English arrived one day: "I'd like to reserve a single room with breakfast for the nights of September 17 and 18. I'll be arriving at 5:00 P.M. by taxi." I translated it for Mother.

The woman appeared at the appointed time with one suitcase, peering out from under a wide-brimmed hat with a ribbon.

"It's a pleasure to have a visitor from so far away," Mother said in Japanese. "We've put you in our best room." Foreign guests were rare at the Iris, and Mother was unusually hospitable. "I'm afraid I'm not much good with languages, but my daughter speaks a little English, so feel free to ask her if you need anything." I don't know whether the woman understood what Mother said, but she smiled brightly as she took off her hat and ran her hand through her brown hair. She was slender, with long arms and legs, and her dress was very simple. Then there was an awkward moment—"as though the air had been let out of the room"—and it dawned on us that the woman was blind.

"I've always wanted to stay at a hotel that bears my name. Now I wonder if I could ask you to explain the layout of the building and take me to my room? Then I can manage on my own." Her English was quite easy to understand.

"Of course," I said. Mother was nudging me, so I began describing the hotel as best I could.

Mother leaned against the front desk and stared at the woman. She frowned and pressed her finger to her temple. There was no sign of the welcoming smile she'd worn a moment ago, and when I finished my explanation, the key she handed the woman was not for the best room but for the smallest one with the worst ventilation, least reliable plumbing, and no view.

The woman thanked me politely when I carried her bag upstairs for her. I wanted to tell her she should let me know if she needed anything, but I realized I couldn't say this in English. She had just taken off her hat, so instead of speaking, I guided her hand to the hook on the wall. The ribbon on the hat added a touch of color to the somber room.

I stood for a moment in front of the hat. The woman's pale blue eyes had an unearthly beauty, as if they weren't eyes at all.

"Why didn't you put her in 301?" I asked Mother when I got back to the desk. "We have plenty of empty rooms."

"Don't be stupid," Mother hissed, keeping her voice low as if to remind me that the woman could hear even if she couldn't see. "What difference does it make if she has an ocean view or not?"

Miss Iris surveyed the hotel from one end to the other, counting the steps in each staircase, pacing out the length of each hall, memorizing the location of the dining room. With her fingers she took in even the tiniest details—light switches, dusty picture frames, door hinges, curtains and sashes, gashes on the banisters, peeling wallpaper. . . . All these things we had long since forgotten she gathered up one by one in her hands, caressing and warming them until they came back to life. It was as if she had come in place of the goddess of the rainbow to offer her grace and affection. She was perhaps the only one who ever truly loved the Hotel Iris.

I had promised the translator that I would have lunch with him, and he had made a reservation at the fanciest restaurant in town, a place I had never been. Thanks to Mother, I didn't have to worry about my hair. I would have liked to have added a ribbon, but I didn't want her wondering why I needed to be so dressed up to go see the old woman.

I decided to wear my yellow dress with the little flowers. It was old, but it was the only good one I had. My purse was cheap and a bit babyish, my straw hat faded. But my shoes were real leather—they had been left behind by a guest. The address she had written in the guest book was fake, so we had no way to send them on to her. "Just keep them," Mother had said. Except for being a bit tight in the toes, they were perfect.

Before slipping out the door, I crept over to Mother's dressing table. There were several lipsticks scattered about. They all seemed too bright, but I chose one, thinking I could use just a tiny bit. The tip was worn to the exact shape of Mother's lips. I touched it to my mouth, releasing its forbidden scent. My heart beat faster. I wondered whether the maid felt like this when she was stealing from me. I drew it across my mouth, pressing as lightly as I could, but when I looked in the mirror, I saw that my lips had become an indecent gash in my face. Rubbing them with a tissue only made matters worse, and I was petrified that Mother would walk in and catch me. I had to leave soon if I was going to be on time, so I made another desperate attempt to apply the lipstick, as though the translator's deepest desire was that I would do this skillfully for him.

I was afraid to disappoint him. He had approached me so timidly, with such caution, that I feared what would happen if I didn't turn out to be exactly what he was hoping for.

I managed at last to get the lipstick right. Then I put on my stockings and my hat and checked one more time to be sure my dress was properly fastened. Someone else was headed for the exact same spot, on the same day, at the same hour. It was an insignificant point, but it made me happy.

Mother and the maid were cleaning rooms on the third floor. I called good-bye to them, ran across the courtyard to the kitchen door, and kept running until I reached the flower clock in the plaza.

"So my letter reached you safely?" the translator asked.

"Yes, of course."

"I was terribly worried that it would be intercepted or go astray before you got a chance to read it." He reached over and tilted back the brim of my hat just a bit, as if to get a better look at my face, and the bright summer sun made me squint. Behind us, the boy was playing his accordion.

"Are you hungry?" he asked. I nodded, though I had no idea whether I was or not. I took him in with my eyes and ears and skin, studying him, and I had no interest in my stomach.

We walked along the shore road toward the restaurant. Beach umbrellas had been planted in the sand. The seawall was exposed, and people were picking their way among the rocks. The street was crowded with tourists who had come up from the beach for lunch. They had thrown on T-shirts over wet, sandy bathing suits, and some were clutching inner tubes. We walked closer together to avoid being separated.

The translator was wearing a wool suit and the same tie as before. Tiny pearls decorated his cuff links and the matching tiepin.

"I've never eaten in a real restaurant," I told him. "Much less such a fancy one."

"There's nothing to be nervous about. Just order whatever you like."

"Do you go often?"

"No, not really. Only when my nephew comes to visit."

"You have a nephew?"

"He's the son of my late wife's younger sister. He's a few years older than you." I was surprised to learn that he had a family, but the words "late wife" struck me most.

"The wall is completely exposed today," he said. Then he pointed out at the sea. Its color was most beautiful at this time of year, the pale blue at the shore deepening gradually out in the open water, set off by the occasional flash of white from a sail or the wake of a ship. The sun bathed the seawall right to its base, glistening on the crust of shells and seaweed, still damp from the retreating tide. I followed his gaze out to sea, finding no place for a "late wife" in a scene like this.

At the restaurant, the doorman smiled and bowed politely, and we were just about to enter when someone spoke up behind us.

"Well, this is a nice surprise!" The voice was familiar. "How are you? I never got a chance to thank you for the other night." The tone was high and sweet, but there was a subtle note of confrontation. The translator put his arm around my shoulders and tried to pass inside without acknowledging the woman. "Now don't pretend you don't remember me," she said, winking significantly at a second woman who had come up with her. "That's too cruel."

Their faces were round and without makeup; their ratty hair was tied up in back. They wore very short skirts, and their feet were bare. I realized that the one who had spoken was the woman who had been at the Iris that night.

"You're a very funny man," she cackled. "Acting all proper. You were happy enough that night with your tongue up my ass!" People passing in the street turned to look, and the customers in the windows of the restaurant stared at us. The smile had faded from the doorman's face. I turned away and clung to the translator's arm.

He sighed so softly that no one else could hear. Then he looked straight ahead as if he hadn't heard her, slipped his arm behind my back, and pushed through the glass door.

"So you're on to little girls now?" she called after us, refusing to give up. "What are you planning to do with her? Young lady! You'd better watch out!" I tried to press deeper into his chest to shut out her voice.

The maître d' greeted us just inside the door. He seemed confused by the women who had practically followed us into the restaurant, but he tried to observe the usual formalities. The translator gave his name. Outside the window, the woman yelled one last insult and stalked away. But her presence lingered around us like a mist.

The maître d' took a long time studying the leather-bound reservations book. His eyes ran from the top of the page to the bottom and back to the top again, and from time to time he stole a glance in our direction. I was feeling more and more uneasy, and I suddenly felt too poorly dressed for the restaurant. I hid my little purse behind my back.

At last the man looked up. "I'm terribly sorry," he began cautiously. "We have no reservation in that name."

"But you must be mistaken," the translator protested. "Could you check again?"

"But I have checked."

"I called five days ago: party of two, July eighth at twelve thirty, a table with a view of the sea."

"I'm afraid there must have been some sort of misunderstanding."

"A misunderstanding?"

"I'm terribly sorry."

"But we're here now. You must be able to do something."

"Unfortunately, we're completely booked."

A drop of sweat appeared on the translator's forehead and traced a line down his temple. His lips were dry, and the hand on my back was cold. The maître d' bowed, but his expression seemed more annoyed than apologetic.

"I want you to get the person who takes your reservations, and we'll clear this up. You can't just pretend I never called. I remember the voice, and every word that was said, down to the last syllable. I want to talk to the person who answers the phone. Or would you rather just show me that book? What would you do if I found my name there in the column for twelve thirty?"

A man who seemed to be the manager appeared from the

back with one of the waiters. Every eye in the restaurant was watching us now. I was frightened more than ever before, and I froze, feeling that something awful would happen if I moved any part of my body.

"How can I help you?" the new man said.

"You can stop insulting us!" the translator shouted. His hand shot out from behind my back and grabbed the reservations book, throwing it violently to the floor. We all stood staring down at the book. The translator was gasping, his empty hand dangling at his side. He seemed to be trying to expel something—not so much his anger as some deep distress. It was as if a tiny crack had opened somewhere in him and was growing, tearing him to pieces. If he had simply been angry, I might have found a way to calm him, but I had no idea how to put him back together once he came apart.

"Please!" I said at last. "We don't have to eat here. Who cares whether there was a reservation or not? Let's go. Please don't make it worse." I clung to him, tears in my eyes. I thought about the sound of the translator's voice as he'd said "Stop insulting us!" It was the voice that had overwhelmed me that night at the Iris. A blade of clear light cutting through the confusion.

I was confused and afraid, and yet somewhere deep inside I was praying that voice would someday give me an order, too.

We had been turned away, and though the color of the sea and the brilliance of the sun hadn't changed, there was no way to regain the excitement we'd felt before the restaurant. It was as though we had suddenly fallen into a cold, dark cave.

"I'm sorry," the translator said. He seemed to have recovered quickly from the embarrassment. The sweat on his brow had dried, and his arm was once again wrapped around my back.

"You mustn't apologize," I said. But my tears would not stop. The woman's insults, the way we had been treated at the restaurant, the sudden change that had come over the translator—and the discovery of my secret desire—were all too much for me.

"I'm sorry you had to see that. I had no idea we'd run into her."

"Please don't apologize."

"Then at least let me wipe away these tears," he said, taking a perfectly pressed handkerchief from his pocket and touching it to my cheek.

"It was just an unfortunate mishap, and that's not why I'm crying." His scent on the handkerchief made me cry all the harder.

No one had said a word as we left the restaurant. The patrons had cast only quick looks of contempt our way, then returned to their meals and conversations as though nothing had happened. The maître d' retrieved the reservations book from the floor and wiped its cover. The doorman held the door open for us as we left.

We walked until the restaurant was out of sight and then

sat on the concrete breakwater, waiting for my tears to sub-side. The sky was cloudless and the sun burned bright. A breeze tugged at the hem of my dress. From time to time, the translator peered sheepishly under the brim of my hat. He patted my back and refolded his handkerchief and brushed the sand from my shoes to pass the time.

A beach ball sailed over the breakwater and rolled at our feet. A small boy, his face smeared with ice cream, was eye-ing us dubiously. Some young people in wet suits left a damp trail as they made their way down the street, and the horn of the excursion boat sounded as it pulled away from the wharf.

"What would you like to do now?" the translator said. I took a deep breath and waited for the last tears to dry.

"I'm hungry," I confessed. Before the restaurant, I'd been too unsettled to eat, but now, after all that had happened, I found myself famished.

"Of course you are! It's past one o'clock. We'll find some-thing delicious—there are plenty of other restaurants. So, tell me, what would you like?"

"That," I said, pointing at the shabby pizza stand directly in front of me.

"But there are much better places. I know a very good restaurant right near here."

"No, this is fine," I said, my finger still pointing at the stand. I had an overwhelming desire to eat greasy pizza, to stuff myself to bursting, and this seemed like the right place for the two of us.

We stood at one end of the counter, eating pizza and sipping Cokes. The translator nibbled the end of his slice, his head cocked to the side in deep thought. When the least bit of grease touched his hand, he wiped it with a paper napkin, which he would then ball up and toss in the ashtray. From time to time he looked up as if about to say something, but he would take another sip of cola instead. I ate slice after slice in silence, my toes throbbing in my secondhand shoes.

The wooden counter, sticky with oil and tomato sauce and Tabasco, was even more scratched and worn down than the front desk at the Iris. A cloud of cigarette smoke hung in the shadows under the awning, and a surly waiter shuffled among the rickety tables. Tiny roaches skittered over the condiments.

Melted cheese stuck to my teeth, and the mushrooms burned my mouth. The lipstick I had applied so carefully that morning was completely gone.

We stepped ashore from the excursion boat and walked along the coast road, away from the tourists headed for the diving shop. At the very end was a small cove, on the shore of which stood the translator's house.

It was a modest structure with a green roof. The lawn was neatly trimmed and the deck freshly painted. White lace curtains hung in the windows, but here and there were signs of decay on the house. The walls and doors and window frames were deeply scarred from long years in the salt air. Concrete stairs encrusted with shells led up to the front door.

"Watch your step," he said, taking my hand as I climbed them. The pain in my toes, forced into the leather shoes, was almost unbearable. But it was not real pain.

"What a beautiful room," I said as I sat down on the

couch. But I didn't mean it. The moment I had walked through the door, something had oppressed me.

"Thank you," he said, apparently genuinely pleased. The gloomy expression he had worn since the restaurant faded at last, and he smiled pleasantly, perhaps considering when to give his first order.

The room served as both parlor and office. One wall was covered with bookshelves. Through a door, I could see a smaller room with a dresser and a bed. The kitchen was also visible through a sliding door that had been left open. The utensils and appliances were old but neat and clean.

There were no decorations to be seen, no pictures or vases or art on the walls. Only things that could be put to use. But the translator had brought to the house a rigid sense of order unlike anything I'd seen before. The spines of the books on the shelves were perfectly aligned, the gas heater was polished to a bright shine, and every wrinkle had been smoothed from the cover on the bed. The room was stuffy, not cozy, and it made me feel I should return the cushion I had propped on my knees to its original place on the couch.

"Would you like something to drink?" he asked, hurrying off to the kitchen. When he reappeared, the teapot, cups, kettle, and creamer were arranged on a tray with the same care as the room itself.

I watched as he warmed the cups, measured the tea, and filled the pot with boiling water. Then he covered the pot and waited. He added milk to each cup, uncovered the pot, and held it high above the cups to pour. The long stream of tea frothed into the milk. Removing the lid from the sugar bowl, he finished his little ritual by giving the cup a half-turn in my direction.

This was the first time I noticed the exquisite movement of his fingers. They were not particularly strong—almost delicate, in fact—spotted with moles and freckles; the fingernails were dark. But when they began to move, they bewitched anything they touched, casting a spell that demanded submission.

I took a sip of tea and looked out the window. A scuba-diving boat cut across the inlet. The town was obscured behind the sparkling waves. A small brown bird flitted down to the deck for a moment and then flew away.

Then I noticed his desk—old and plain, with the tools of his trade neatly arranged on top: five sharp pencils, two well-worn dictionaries, a paperweight, a magnifying glass, a letter opener, various thick books. One notebook lay open, and the writing on the page was as precise as the arrangement on the desk. The tiny characters had been copied out perfectly, with no changes or corrections.

"Is this the novel about Marie?" I asked. I reached out for the book, but he stopped my hand. Perhaps he didn't want me to touch his things, or perhaps he simply wanted to touch me.

"That's right," he said.

It was the first time I'd seen Russian writing.

"Russian is interesting to look at, even if you don't understand it," I said.

"And why is that?"

"It's like a code meant for keeping romantic secrets." He was still holding my hand. "What is Marie up to these days?" I asked.

"She has finally met the riding master. They are embracing in a corner of the stable. He has his riding crop in his hand. A horse whinnies softly, shaking its halter. Straw rustles at their feet. A ray of sunlight cuts through the darkness, and then they . . ." He drew me close and pressed his mouth to mine. I could feel the warmth of his lips and the rough parching of old age. It was a quiet kiss. Even the sound of the waves outside had stopped, and the silence seemed to draw us in.

His desire grew bit by bit. His hands wandered from my shoulders to my hips, lingering at each bone and rib along the way. I didn't know how to respond—I could only obey him.

I didn't know whether the things the translator did to my body were normal, nor how to find out. But I suspected they were special, different from the pictures I would imagine at the front desk of the Iris when the secret night noises drifted down from the rooms.

Then, at last, he said it.

"Take off your clothes."

It was the first order he gave me, and I trembled at the thought that this voice was now speaking only to me. I shook my head, not to refuse but to hide the trembling. "Take everything off," he said. Desire and impatience stirred under his calm expression. He had been as timid as usual all day—until we reached the island, where his rule over me began.

"No," I said, crossing the room and trying to open the door. The teacups he had set out for us rattled.

"Do you want to leave?" I had not noticed him move, but he was standing in front of the door when I reached it. He took hold of my wrist. "There's half an hour until the next boat." Pain slowly quivered through my wrist as his fingertips dug into the skin. I found it hard to believe that a small man of his age could be so strong. But I knew he was going to hold me here, that I could not leave this place.

"Let me go," I said. The words that came out of my mouth were the opposite of what I wanted, but I knew that resisting would make his orders even more forceful. He tried to drag me back to the center of the room, but he pulled so violently on my arm that we both fell. I caught a glimpse of the leg of the couch, a stray slipper, the sea through a gap in the curtains.

"I'll show you how," he said. Pressing my face to the floor, he ripped open my dress. There was a tearing sound, as if he had slit my back with a knife, and I tried to curl into a ball. But he refused to let me move, not a finger, not an eyelid.

He was still terribly angry, and, in his own way, he was using my body to take revenge on that woman and the maître d'. My ear was flattened, my breasts crushed, my mouth forced half open. The pile of the carpet had a bitter taste. My whole body should have hurt, but I didn't feel anything. Somehow, my nerves had become hopelessly tangled, so that pain became vaguely pleasurable as it rippled over my skin.

He tore off my dress and threw it aside—a ball of yellow

crumpled in the corner. Then in quick succession, my slip and stockings and bra were stripped away. He seemed to know exactly what to unfasten, where to pull. His arms and legs and fingers moved skillfully and relentlessly over me. When he finally slipped my panties down to my ankles, I let out a cry. It was then that I realized I was no more than a helpless lump of flesh.

I wanted to scream at the top of my lungs, but I could only moan. He forced my head deeper into the carpet. I caught sight of the Russian books in the bookcase—and my ugly reflection in the glass front.

I was certain he would be disappointed by my under-developed breasts, my sweaty pubic patch, by the stubble under my arms and the ugly color of my private parts. How could he admire the hideous shape of my body when he tied me up? Wouldn't he have preferred the woman outside the restaurant, even with her insults?

He produced a strange piece of cord from somewhere and began to tie me up. It was thicker and stronger and more flexible than the plastic twine they use at the post office, and it had a slightly medicinal smell, like the science labs at school. Or perhaps it smelled like my grandfather before he died, like the tube that had drained the yellow fluid from his stomach.

The cord dug into my flesh, holding me fast. The transla-tor was remarkably skillful, quick and sure.

I looked at my reflection in the glass front of the bookcase. My wrists were bound behind my back. The cord crushed my breasts, but the nipples were sensitive and pink and wanting to be caressed. The cord ran down between my thighs and around my knees, spreading me wide open, and if I made any effort to close my legs, it dug deeper into the soft place between them. Light fell in this crease, this pleat of skin that had been hidden in the dark until now.

Then he lay on top of me. He moved very slowly, as if to make his pleasure last as long as possible—and to be absolutely sure the cords did not come loose. His lips ran over my neck and ears, and then pressed against mine. It was not quite a kiss, not like the one he had given me a few minutes earlier. Our mouths met, and saliva, tinged with the flavor of cheese from the pizza, dripped into me. He played with my breasts. They were swollen and sensitive from the cords.

He was still in his suit and tie. Even his cuff links were still neatly fastened. He looked exactly as he did when we met in front of the flower clock—though I was now completely changed.

He used only his lips and tongue and fingers, but they were enough. Nothing was neglected; I felt I was learning for the first time that I had shoulder blades and temples, ankles and earlobes and an anus. He caressed me, moistening each part with his tongue, tasting me with his lips.

I closed my eyes. That way, I could feel the humiliation more deeply. The vinyl on the couch rubbed against my back. I should have been chilled, but I started to sweat.

His mouth probed between my legs. Even his breath made my nerves cry out. I felt as though I was being torn apart, split between fear of what he would do next and the desire to be shamed even more. But out of the tear, pleasure came bubbling like blood from a wound.

He opened the folds one by one, his tongue playing over the tiny seed under the last layer. I cried out and tried to twist away, but he refused to release me. The little mound twitched nervously in the damp pleats.

His fingers ventured into me. It had started at last. There, between my legs, everything seemed to be coming to pieces. I tried to close myself, terrified that everything would dis-integrate, fly apart from the pleasure. But the cords held me fast.

He pushed deeper into the darkness, touching places I had never reached myself. His fingers twisted between warm folds of flesh.

"Stop!" I screamed at last. He slapped me, flooding my head with a new kind of pain. I thought of Marie in the stable, the riding master, the riding crop.

He wiped my cheek with the fingers that had been inside me a moment before, streaking it with something sticky.

It was hot outside but cold here, not because I was naked but from the dull chill in the room. The south-facing win-dow had been left open, and the curtain fluttered from time to time, but the hot breeze never reached me. The scene outside the window seemed to come from a distant world— the painted deck, the lawn, the sea spreading out beyond. We were alone.

"Do you like it?" he asked. I moved my chin, not sure

whether I did or not, and past caring. "I'm sure you do," he said, suddenly forcing four fingers into my mouth. I gagged, trying to keep from vomiting. "Does it taste good?" he said. Saliva dribbled from the corner of my mouth. "It's so good you're drooling!" I nodded. "Slut!" he muttered, slapping me again.

"It feels so good," I said. "Do it more, please."

He grabbed my hair and dragged me to the couch. I tried to cover my head with my arms, but he was quick and strong. Mother's neat bun fell in my face, the pins sticking out here and there.

"Don't resist, understand?" Despite the pain, his voice thrilled me. I tried to nod, but I could barely move my head. "Answer me!"

"Yes," I managed to murmur.

"Louder!"

"Yes, I understand." We repeated this exchange over and over until he seemed satisfied.

He didn't seem to trust me yet, though I had given up trying to get away and did exactly as I was told. He was determined to strip me of every last trace of freedom.

"Why are you trembling?" He took hold of my chin, but even this slight motion caused the cord to tighten and bind. I needed to give him the answer he wanted, but I could only manage a sigh. He pulled harder on the knot at the back of my neck, sending a wave of pain through my body.

"I'm sorry." Roused by the pain, I managed to speak at last, but he didn't relax his grip. "I'm sorry. Forgive me."

They were words I had said over and over to my mother since childhood. Though I'd had no idea what forgiveness meant, I had cried for it nonetheless. But now, finally, I understood. From the bottom of my heart I wanted to be forgiven. "Forgive me, please. I beg you. I won't move again. I'll be quiet."

He looked down at me, studying my body with his un-blinking stare. In this room where everything was arranged in perfect order—from the dish cupboard and bedspread to the desk and the tiny characters in the notebook—I was an affront to order. My dress and underwear were strewn about, my ugly body was draped over the couch. Reflected in the glass, I looked like a dying insect, like a chicken trussed up in the butcher's storeroom.

The sun was disappearing into the sea when I got back to the Iris. Showers were running in several rooms—guests cleaning up after a day at the beach. Swimsuits were drying outside the windows in the courtyard. The light of the sunset dyed red the curls of the boy with the harp.

"What have you done to your hair?" Mother noticed immediately that something was odd.

"It caught on my hat," I said, trying to sound natural.

"Well, it's a mess. You can't work at the desk like that." She dragged me off to the dressing table and put up my hair exactly as she had that morning, despite the fact that I would soon be taking it down again for my bath. I worried she would be able to tell what the man had done, but I also knew she wouldn't. I had gone somewhere far away today. Far away over the sea, to a place she could never reach.

We had tried to fix my hair in his bathroom.

"No, that's not it. She's going to be furious."

"But it's very pretty," he said, trying to console me.

"Mother is insane about my hair. She'll notice even one pin out of place."

His bathroom was insane in its own way, each surface carefully polished, from the sink to the mirror in the medicine chest. The old-fashioned faucet with no hot-water knob, the razor blades and toothbrush, the new bar of soap.

His comb was too fine for my thick hair, and we had no camellia oil. I tried to tie it up while he gingerly stroked my neck, afraid to get in the way. He was suddenly timid again, plucked out of our private world and returned to normal. But I knew how I had looked and felt just a few moments before. As I carefully replaced each pin, I wondered when the storm would come again.

"You are so lovely," he said, speaking to my reflection in the mirror. Then he put his hands on my hips and drew me gently to him. It was a simple gesture, but it thrilled me as much as his tongue running over my naked body. It made us terribly sad to part.

"Well, I don't want you wearing a hat anymore," Mother said. "Why should you hide such a pretty face?" He had said almost the same thing. "I've told you before, you should show off your hair. You can spend all kinds of money on clothes and makeup, but your beautiful hair is free."

We could hear guests in the lobby, probably on their way out to dinner. Someone put a room key on the front desk; children were arguing. Mother pulled so hard on my hair that my eyes watered, but it didn't hurt at all.

In my heart, I told her that her pretty little Mari had become the ugliest person in the whole world.

The slip I was wearing that day has disappeared. I had hidden it at the bottom of a drawer full of underwear. So why did she take that, of all things? It was cheap, and the lace was in tatters from so many washings. But she doesn't care—she seems to need the thrill of taking things from me.

Perhaps she put it on and admired herself in the mirror before coming to work. She's quite thin, though she eats well enough. Her jaw is pointed, her arms and legs are like twigs, and her ribs stick out—a body suited for stolen underwear. But I didn't really care that she took it. He tore it off me in an instant and tossed it under the couch. It was useless—there was no need for such things between the translator and me.

The summer season had begun in earnest now, and we were busy at the Iris. The rooms were full almost every day. Guests would check in, have their swim, stroll along the seawall, sleep in our beds—and then check out again. The maid, our resident thief, began coming to help out in the evenings as well as during the day.

A letter from the translator arrived every three days. The handwriting and the polite words were always the same—and so different from the way he had treated me that day. I enjoyed reading his formal, almost humble, letters and remembering what had happened at his house. When I finished reading them, I would mix them with the trash from the guest rooms and burn them in the incinerator in the backyard. I would have liked to keep them, but there was no safe hiding place in the Iris, no place Mother or the maid wouldn't find them.

As we got busier, it became harder to find time alone at the front desk. Mother would constantly call for my help, and the vacationing guests were demanding—ice for a sunburn, a drain plugged with sand, rooms that were too cold or too hot, mosquitoes, a taxi to be called. . . . There seemed no end to their orders and requests, but I tended to them all without a word. I felt it was important to be quiet, and to keep my secret safe.

A little after noon one day, I went up to change the towels in 202. The young couple staying in the room had just taken their baby down to the beach. Their suitcases lay open, overflowing with disposable diapers, jars of baby food, dirty socks, makeup bags. Powdered milk had spilled from a baby bottle tipped over on the night table. We had squeezed a crib into the small room, and there was barely space to walk. The curtains were faded from the afternoon sun, the wallpaper peeling here and there. I was about to put fresh towels in the bathroom when I remembered that the translator had been here in Room 202. Though not for the whole night.

I wondered whether he had done the same things to that woman he had done to me. Though they had no bags, had he brought that strange cord with him? Did he tie up the woman on the bed by the window or the bed by the wall? Did he order her to lay on the narrow strip of floor?

She was plumper than me, so the cord would have sunk deeper into her flesh. Here in this room, which smelled of sweat and perfume and baby formula. She had put on a good show, gasping with fake desire, flicking her tongue and grasping with her fingers.

I was not the only one who had been loved in this way, not the translator's only victim. I was jealous of that woman.

Having hung the clean towels on the rack, I closed the bathroom door. I picked up a scrap of paper and threw it in the wastebasket, then I sat down on the edge of the bed. A letter had just arrived, and I was desperate to read it.

. . . my heart beats faster at the thought of you climbing my shell-covered stairs, drinking tea from my teacup, peering in my mirror. I find myself stopping to caress that mirror, my hand still covered in shaving cream.

Anyone who saw me would think me odd indeed, but those with impoverished hearts cannot recognize simple miracles, even the sort revealed in the act of shaving.

When they turned us away from the restaurant, I wasn't worried about my lunch—I was worried I had lost you. That's why I was so furious. That woman was there when we first met, and she reappeared when we were about to share our first meal. But you saved me, you protected me with a warmth I had never felt before.

On the surface, my life hasn't changed. I rise at 7:00, and I translate for three hours before lunch and two after. When I finish work, I go for a walk around the island and then take a nap. After that, I make my dinner. I am at home alone in the evening, and go to bed at 11:00. No one comes to visit, not the mailman, or the bill collector, or even a salesman. But now this sad existence is filled with joy at the knowledge that I have met you—and with the fear and regret that joy brings with it.

I ask myself what would become of me if something happened to you, if you were struck by a car and disappeared without a word. Or perhaps it was all just a dream, perhaps there was no girl named Mari, not there in the plaza, not at the Hotel Iris. That's what I fear most. . . .

The stronger my feelings for you become, the greater my fear, and the more freely I abandon myself to baseless speculations and anxieties. Yet the more I immerse myself in the profound joy of loving you.

I beg of you to go on living in this world I inhabit. I suppose you find this a rather ridiculous request, but to me it is of the utmost importance that you simply exist.

"What are you doing in here?" I looked up to find that I had left the door ajar and the maid was peering in at me.

"Nothing," I said, jumping to my feet. The envelope fell to the floor.

"You have no business in here."

"I forgot to change the towels," I said, picking up the envelope. I tried to slip the letter back inside, but I was too nervous to manage it.

"Liar. I saw you just sitting there on the bed." She reached out for the letter with a nasty laugh. "What have you got there?"

"Nothing," I said, trying to stuff the envelope in my pocket. She grabbed my wrist and snatched the letter, nearly tearing it in half. "Please, stop."

"What are you hiding? Surely it can't hurt if I read just a few lines." We fought for the letter in that cramped room, scattering diapers and baby bottles, and she laughed and taunted me as she danced away, brandishing the letter over her head.

"Let's see . . . 'My Dear Mari, I hope you have not caught cold. Dear Mari, just writing the words makes me impossibly happy' . . . It's a love letter!" she cried.

"You're horrible, reading someone else's mail."

"And what about you, hiding up here to get out of work. But who is it from? He's no spring chicken, to judge from the handwriting. But this is a nice touch—a woman's name in the return address. Who came up with that bright idea?"

"Please stop!"

"Oh! Now I remember, you're supposed to be writing to some rich old lady. But this is obviously a man. Tell me all about him. I want to know everything!" She was hopping up and down, beside herself with glee.

"I won't tell you anything. It's none of your concern."

"But you're like a daughter to me, and this is serious business for a girl your age. I'll have to tell your mother, but you know how upset she'll be. She gets so crazy about anything that has to do with her Mari . . ."

"Give me back the slip," I blurted out. She fell silent and her face went blank.

"What are you talking about?" she said, her voice trembling just a bit. "You do say the oddest things."

"Don't pretend you don't know," I said. "My compass, my handkerchief, the stockings, the petticoat, my little beaded purse—I want it all back." I had nearly forgotten about these things, and yet the list came spilling out. She bit her lip. "All I have to do is tell Mother and she'll fire you. And if everyone in town finds out you're a kleptomaniac, no one will hire you ever again."

Snorting in disgust, she crumpled the letter, threw it on the floor, and stalked out of the room. I picked it up and went to burn it in the yard.

Summer vacation had begun, and the school was deserted. The sky above the empty bicycle rack was slowly turning crimson, and the rays of the setting sun slanted deep into the classroom, lighting up the tables, the blackboard, the beakers, and the translator's face.

"Do you do that often?" I asked, picking up an eraser someone had left behind and rolling it across the lab table.

"Do what?" he said.

"Spend the night with someone you don't know. . . ." I spoke slowly, choosing my words. He looked down at the worn eraser and said nothing. I studied his expression, worried I had offended him, but he gave no hint of displeasure. Perhaps he was simply searching for the best way to answer.

"Not often," he said, after a long pause. "It's actually quite rare."

"How did you meet her?"

"She was standing on a corner waiting for customers, so I spoke to her."

"But how did you know she was a whore? They don't wear signs, do they?"

He looked up and frowned. "You just know," he said. "A woman like that is always hunting for a man—that's why she's out on the street."

It had been amazingly easy to get into the classroom. The lock was broken on the back gate, just as it had been when I was a student here. From there, we cut behind the pool, past the archery range and the tennis courts, and up the fire escape next to the music room. The science room was the last one on the second floor. We hadn't seen anyone or heard a sound.

After spending the afternoon at his house, we had intended to say good-bye at the dock on the island. But neither of us could bear to part so soon, and he had ended up riding the excursion boat with me back to the mainland. Then, after the boat reached shore, we wandered around town while he waited for the next boat to take him back, and ended up at the school.

"I get terribly frightened sometimes," he said. "When I finish a job, I take the boat to town to mail it off—it might be a pamphlet advertising pills made from sturgeon fat . . . 'just ten tablets a day improves circulation and strengthens the liver.' I buy a stamp and drop it in the box. The envelope makes just the slightest sound as it falls, and at that moment a terrible fear comes over me." He reached out and drew an alcohol burner toward him. The curve of the lamp fit perfectly in his palm; the wick snaked through the glass. "It's not a matter of being sad or lonely. I no longer feel lonely. No, it's as though I'm being sucked silently into some hole in the atmosphere, to disappear altogether. Pulled in by an overwhelming force, and once I'm gone, I'll never get back."

"Do you mean you'd die?"

"No, everyone dies. This is something else, like being drawn toward an invisible chasm. I feel I'm being singled out for some sort of punishment. In fact, I'm afraid I won't be permitted to die but be forced to wander eternally at the ends of the earth. No one will mourn me, or even so much as notice that I'm gone. No one will look for me, except perhaps the sturgeon pill company wanting to pay my translation fee—and they would give up soon, over such a paltry sum as translators are paid." He stared at his reflection in the glass of the lamp. His hand moved, and the reflection wavered with the shifting liquid.

"I pay these women to help me escape this fear. The desires of the flesh confirm my existence. And then, in the morning, I take the first boat back to the island. I throw out the notes for the sturgeon translation, the sample pamphlets, even the blotter I'd been using—and then I'm sure that the crisis has passed."

I nodded. I hadn't understood everything that he'd said, but I didn't want to disturb the quiet of the classroom. He breathed a long sigh, as though his fear had finally left him.

The wind off the ocean had died at dusk. The leaves on the trees were still, and the school flag and the nets on the soccer goals hung limp. We went into the storage room at the back of the classroom. It was dark and stuffy and its shelves were filled with equipment for high school science experiments: flasks, beakers, mortars, a scale and weights, a chart with the periodic table, a slide projector, a model of the human skeleton, test tubes, microscopes, insect specimens, petri dishes. . . . We walked down the narrow aisle between the shelves. The air was faintly medicinal, like the translator's plastic cord.

"Did you think me contemptible?" he asked.

"No," I said. "I've known about these women since I was a child. They come to the Iris all the time." A specimen box caught my eye; the pin inside had come loose, and the beetle lay at the bottom.

"Do you do the same things to them?" I asked.

"They could never be the same," he said, shaking his head. "Mari . . ." I loved the sound of my name on his lips. "There is no one like you. You are unique, every fingernail, every strand of hair incomparable."

I didn't know how to answer—I just wanted him to say my name over and over. There was no need for other words, words that had a meaning. I opened and closed the drawers under the shelves at random, test tubes rattling together.

Earlier that same day, I had been tied to a bed with iron rails that were ideal for securing my ankles and wrists. He had cut away my slip with a large pair of scissors. The blades had been sharpened to a fine edge, and the steel had a dark sheen. He snapped them open and closed in the air, as if to test the sharpness and savor the sound. Then he drew them straight up my body from my spread legs, and the slip fell away as if by magic.

The blades touched my abdomen. A cold shock ran through me, and my head began to spin. If he had pressed just a bit harder, the scissors might have pierced my soft belly. The skin would have peeled back, the fat beneath laid bare. Blood would have dripped on the bedspread.

My head had been filled with premonitions of fear and pain. I wondered whether his wife had died like this. But as these premonitions became realities, pleasure also erupted violently in me. I knew now how I reacted at such a moment: my body grew moist and liquid.

He cut the shoulder straps on my slip with great care. I knew it was futile, but I continued to wiggle my arms and legs to loosen the cords. The bed creaked as I struggled, and that seemed to excite him even more. The remains of the tattered slip fell to the floor—the second one I had lost.

"The last boat will be leaving soon," I said. The horn blew in the distance, and he sighed, as if he had heard the one sound he did not want to hear.

We held each other for a few moments, as we always did to delay the inevitable parting. It was the only way to hold the sadness at bay. Our bodies had melted into each other, cheek to cheek, breath meeting between us.

My blouse was glued to my back—with no slip to absorb the sweat. A faint red mark from the cord was visible on my wrist.

"Why do we have to leave each other? Why do we have to be apart?"

"I don't know. . . ." He shook his head again and again.

It soon became more difficult to slip out of the hotel and see the translator. I was running out of excuses, and there was a limit to the number of times I could visit the "rich old lady." At first Mother had been excited by the word "rich," but her enthusiasm had faded. As soon as she realized there would be nothing tangible for her in the relationship, my imaginary friend became nothing more than an annoying old woman.

"What good does it do you to spend time with her? She should be giving you something for this. She has you come when it suits her, when she's bored. And I'm the one who's inconvenienced—at the busiest time of year. You have to drop her."

The Iris was open year-round, and I had never had a regular day off. If I so much as went next door to buy an ice cream while I was supposed to be watching the desk, Mother got furious. "We'll probably have an empty room tonight, thanks to you and your ice cream," she would tell me. Then she'd take the half-eaten cone out of my hand and toss it in the sink.

I had to pick just the right moment to ask to go out. It was important to avoid inconveniencing her—even if she had nothing more important planned than an evening with her dancing friends, that always took precedence. Until now, my errands had been relatively unimportant, attending a soccer game, returning videos, buying menstrual pads. . . .

But things were different now. I was willing to tell any sort of lie to keep my appointment.

"I have a toothache." I had decided to announce this at lunch, when the maid was with us. I had a feeling it might go more smoothly with her there. "Can I go to the dentist?"

"Which tooth?"

"A molar, on the right."

"How much does it hurt?"

"A lot."

"But the circus arrives tomorrow and every room is booked. How can you have a toothache at a time like this?" She went on muttering for some time. I took a bite of my cucumber sandwich, careful to chew only with the left side of my mouth.

The maid forced half her sandwich into her mouth and washed it down with a sip of beer. She said nothing about my trip to the dentist and avoided looking at me, staring at the crumbs on the table instead. "I'm sorry I won't be able to

help with the rooms," I told her. She grunted noncommittally. "Oh, could you show me that pretty little purse you
had the other day, the beaded one?" I wanted to be sure that
she understood our agreement.

She drained the rest of her beer and threw the empty can
in the trash.

"I don't have it with me today," she said.

"No? Too bad," I said. I picked apart the last sandwich on
the plate and ate the cheese. The maid lit a cigarette. Mother
burped.

It was suffocating, and no breeze ever reached the kitchen.
A fan rattled above the refrigerator, but it did little more
than stir up the hot air. The guests were all down at the beach,
and the hotel was empty. Cicadas cried in the courtyard, and
the sun beat down on the back of the boy playing the harp.
He seemed even more exhausted than usual.

That evening, there was a minor incident in the lobby. A
guest came back drunk and touched my breast.

"Sorry!" he said and laughed obscenely. "That hand's got
a mind of its own."

At first, I hadn't realized what he was doing. I was passing
his key across the desk when his hand shot out and held my
breast for a moment. It took several seconds before I knew
what was happening. Then I screamed and threw the key on
the counter. I rubbed my breast, but that just made him
laugh harder.

"No need to get so worked up, young lady," he said. "It was just a little accident. I didn't mean anything by it." He steadied himself on the counter and fixed me with his blood-shot eyes. His breath reeked of alcohol. Then I screamed again at the top of my lungs.

Mother came running from the back room, and guests peered out from their doorways.

At some point my screams had turned to sobs, and I was crouching behind the desk. But I knew even then that I was overreacting. A drunk had gotten a bit out of line, nothing more.

"Can't you take a joke, missy? Don't be like that." From behind the counter, it sounded as though he had begun to sulk.

"I'm very sorry," I heard Mother say. "You must have star-tled her—she's still just a child. Don't think a thing about it. I'll talk to her. . . . And I'm very sorry we disturbed the rest of you. Please accept my apologies." She was being her usual charming self for the guests. "You," she said, turning back to me and lowering her voice, "will you stop that? He didn't rape you, he just touched your breast. It's nothing, like a fly land-ing on it. If we play our cards right, we might even get a little something out of him tomorrow."

A dead cockroach lay curled up in the dust behind the desk. I wasn't sure why I was crying anymore. It was quiet in the lobby, and I assumed the drunk had left and the other guests had gone back to their rooms. The only sound was Mother's voice prattling on.

It occurred to me that I was crying because I wanted to see the translator. I wanted to feel the warmth of his skin, see the shy smile that lit up his face when he caught sight of me in the crowd. I wanted to repeat our secret ceremony at his home on the island. Though I knew I would see him the next day, that was somehow no comfort as I cried behind the desk. I wanted to see him that instant, and the feeling made me terribly sad.

The maid betrayed me. She did not show up at the Iris at the usual hour.

"She called to ask for the day off. She said she has a stomachache," Mother told me.

"But what about my dentist's appointment?"

"You can go tomorrow. But I've got to have you here today. We're full. What a time to have indigestion!" But tomorrow wouldn't do at all! I had to be in front of the clock in the plaza at two this afternoon. I wanted to scream this at her, but there was nothing I could do but obey in silence. "Well, don't just stand there. When you're done cleaning up in the dining room, you can come help me change beds." Her orders always made me miserable. She beat me down and robbed me of any happiness.

I did the dishes. There were bits of ham with teeth marks to be scraped away, yogurt-coated spoons to be rinsed, leftover coffee to be poured down the drain.

Stragglers were still coming down for breakfast. A woman

with big breasts in shorts and a tank top and a young man in sunglasses ordered an espresso and a tea with lemon. When I told them we only had regular coffee, the woman pursed her lips and the man snorted in disgust. I retrieved the lemon I had just put in the refrigerator and cut a slice. They had an endless stream of requests and complaints: Do you have blueberry jam? The cheese is too hard. Could you reheat the bread? There's something on this knife. . . . A mountain of dirty dishes filled the sink. The glass the woman had used was smeared with pink lipstick, and no matter how much I rubbed it would not come off.

In the lobby, guests were beginning to check out. "Mari!" Mother called my name from somewhere. The cool of the morning had given way to a hot summer sun beating down on the courtyard. Someone was ringing the bell on the front desk. I threw the lipstick-stained glass into the sink, and it shattered with a lovely crystalline crash.

The maid was obviously just pretending to be sick. She must have known I had a date with the man who wrote the letter, and she was trying to prevent me from keeping it. Perhaps she was angry with me for bringing up the beaded purse in front of Mother. Perhaps she wanted to punish me. Or perhaps she simply enjoyed making me suffer.

The translator had no telephone, so I had no way to cancel our appointment. Somehow, I would have to get away from the Iris by two o'clock. I could not disappoint him.

After I had taken care of the guests in the lobby, I hid from Mother and phoned the housekeeper.

"How are you feeling?" I asked.

"It's kind of you to call," she said. Her tone was self-satisfied.

"Perhaps you drank too much beer."

"Maybe—that would do it in this heat."

"Mother's pretty upset."

"She's always upset."

"Why are you pretending to be sick?"

"Who's pretending?" she said. I could tell she was barely able to keep from laughing. "Don't talk nonsense. Why would I lie to get out of work? I don't get paid unless I show up."

"You don't fool me," I said. Mother had turned off the vacuum cleaner. I drew the phone closer and cupped my hand around the receiver. "I know what you're up to. You want to keep me here, keep me from going to the dentist."

"Don't be silly! I couldn't care less about your dentist. You can go see him or not, it's all the same to me." I could hear ice clinking in a glass and then the sound of swallowing. She was eating and drinking, and she wasn't even trying to hide it from me. "And how would you know whether I'm faking or not? My stomach really does hurt, too much to be cleaning rooms, that's for sure. Besides, your mother told me I could stay home—"

"Be here by one thirty," I said, cutting her off.

"I'm sorry, but that's impossible."

"No, listen to me. By one thirty at the very latest."

"And why should I?"

"Because if you aren't, I'll tell Mother. You know what I

mean. And you'll lose more than just a day's pay; you'll lose everything." The vacuum cleaner started up again, but it was quiet at the other end of the line. I was afraid that she would say I could go ahead and tell, that she wanted to be done with us. Or that she would threaten to tell Mother I was meeting a man. I tried to calm myself; everything would be all right. I had burned his letters, so there was no proof. But what she had done was terrible. All I had to do was show Mother my little purse in her bag—or make her undress to reveal my slip. "You have until one thirty," I said, and then I hung up.

It was a terribly busy day, without so much as a moment to eat lunch. The carpets in the rooms were full of sand, and Mother did nothing but scream at me the whole time we were vacuuming. Then the new guests started arriving before we had finished the cleaning. There were lots of calls—the clinic, a landscaper, the travel agency, the dance teacher—and guests canceling, making reservations, bothering me for directions. . . . And on top of everything else, the toilets on the third floor were clogged, and a sickening stench spread through the whole hotel. I called the plumber immediately, but he took forever to arrive. By now I was surrounded by guests shouting complaints at me—the vile smell, the sweltering heat, someone had cut their foot on the rocks. Everything seemed to be my fault.

The problem turned out to be a pair of panties that were stuck in the pipes in Room 301—the room of the couple who had been late to breakfast that morning. They were horrible, indecent panties, exactly the sort that woman would wear, and they emerged as a filthy lump from deep in the pipes.

Now it was getting late. The translator would have left the island and would be on the excursion boat, dressed as always in a starched white shirt, a tie, and the painfully hot suit. I stared at the clock as I apologized to the guests, and thought only of him.

The maid did not seem to be coming. I thought I heard something at the kitchen door, but when I looked out it was only a stray cat.

"I'm starved," Mother said. "I can't do another thing. Go make us lunch." I went back to the kitchen and heated up some canned curry. Guests continued to arrive, so I ate standing in the kitchen door. By the time I got back to the lobby, Mother's curry was cold.

It was nearly 1:30, but there was still no sign of the maid. She seemed determined to punish me. Even if I ran out the door right now, I would still be late. But here I was, eating curry. It was too awful. I forced down the last, cold bite.

"The tablecloths are dirty," Mother said, still on edge despite her lunch. "Go wash them now or they won't be dry tomorrow morning." She slammed the door and went up to check whether things had improved on the third floor.

So I washed the tablecloths. I bleached out the butter and jam and orange juice stains and starched them, and then hung them out to dry in the narrow, mosquito-infested strip of dirt in back of the hotel. Four cloths on the top pole, three on the bottom, perfectly aligned, with the edges folded back exactly seven inches and secured with two clothespins. It had to be exactly seven inches, not six or eight, and exactly two clothespins, never three or one. Those were Mother's orders.

I'm not sure why I was so timid with Mother, why I didn't just throw the tablecloths on the ground and run off to meet the translator. The thought of not seeing him was as unbearable as the thought that Mother would find out. I felt as though I couldn't breathe, as though the air around me was getting thinner by the moment. If only the housekeeper would come, then everything would be all right.

The sight of the clock became unbearable. The hands moved relentlessly, past two o'clock, then three, and my hatred for the maid grew with every turn. I imagined the translator, standing before the accordion player under the merciless sun in the plaza. The coins in the accordion case sparkled, but the tourists never stopped to listen to the boy's sad melody. Only the translator seemed to hear, to give himself over to its melancholy.

He would glance at his watch from time to time. Then he would look down the shore road, blinking in the sunlight, expecting me to come running up to him at any moment. The road was crowded with people, but the one person he wished for did not appear. His eyes moved back and forth from his watch to the flower clock, as if to be absolutely certain of the time.

His mind would run through all sorts of possibilities. Perhaps he had the wrong date. Perhaps I had never received his letter. I may have fallen terribly ill. He turned back to watch the boy and listen to his tune.

I pulled on a tablecloth with all my strength, smoothing out the wrinkles. I couldn't bear to look at the clock anymore. He must have given up by now and returned to the island. I could only hope he hadn't concluded that I hated him. Crouching under the drying poles, I thought of all the sad things that had happened since yesterday. When I pictured the translator, it was sadness I felt, even more than my love for him.

I don't know how long I stayed that way. I could hear Mother's voice in the kitchen. Dishes clattering, chairs scraping, footsteps, quiet laughter. The maid had come!

I wiped my face with the tablecloth hanging in front of me and ran to the kitchen.

"So how are you feeling?"

"I skipped breakfast and lunch, and I feel a lot better."

"You didn't have to come in, you know."

"I thought I'd come and see how I felt."

"Well, I'm grateful. We've been swamped."

She was tying the strings of her apron as she chatted with Mother. Our eyes met for only a second as I poked my head in the kitchen door, but her look said that she'd kept her promise and that I would have to keep mine.

"I'm finished with the tablecloths," I said. "Could I go to the dentist now? It's unbearable." Breaking free from the maid's glare, I turned to go.

SEVEN

"I look awful. . . . You mustn't laugh!" I reached down to fasten the buckle on my sandal and brush the dust from my skirt.

"You look fine." His tone was gentle.

"I ran . . . all the way." I was gasping and found it hard to speak. My blouse was soaked with sweat, the front of my skirt was damp from the tablecloths, and my legs were covered with red welts from the mosquitoes.

"You're more lovely than ever." He put his arm around my shoulders to calm me. This was what I had been craving.

The plaza was still full of people, but the sun had begun to set. The flower clock was half in shadow, and the flagstones that ran along the base of the seawall were disappearing under the waves.

"I'm sorry I'm so late. Have you been waiting the whole time?"

"It doesn't matter."

"I wanted to come, but I couldn't get away. I thought I'd go crazy."

"I hope you didn't do anything rash to get here."

"I said I was going to the dentist, so I have as much time as it would take to fill a cavity."

"Then we'll pretend the dentist was very busy."

He seemed quite calm, and there was no sign that he had been waiting for hours in the heat. His skin was pale, and his necktie was still carefully knotted.

Off the island, he never reproached me, accepting everything without complaint. In that room, however, surrounded by his Russian books, he forgave nothing.

We walked a few blocks from the shore, the surf muffled behind the houses. The street was lined with antiques stores, cafés, camera shops, and hotels that were smaller but nicer than the Iris. The restaurants would soon display their dinner menus for the tourists who had come out to cool their sunburned skin in the evening breeze.

From time to time we caught a glimpse of the sea between the buildings, a thin strip of blue that faded imperceptibly into the sky. As we passed the boatyard, we began to hear music. Signs with red arrows lined the sidewalk, and the trees were hung with twinkling lights and flags from various countries. A group of children ran by.

"It's the circus," I said.

Overnight, a vacant lot next to a storage company had been filled with booths and stalls, a merry-go-round, a teacup ride, a hall of mirrors. Some of the rides were playing music, flying through the air, while others attracted the crowds with bright lights. Everything had been painted in brilliant colors. Neither the sound of the surf nor the light of the setting sun reached the fairground. The translator reached for my hand, and together we walked in. A clown greeted us and took our tickets.

A round stage had been set up at the front of the lot and decorated like a cake, and on it an odd-looking band was playing. At first I thought it was some sort of giant music box with life-size dolls playing the instruments, but on closer inspection I could see the dolls were real people. We watched for a while. The trombone player winked at me. The stage turned around and around as they played. The tempo was lively, but they were playing in a minor key—an odd piece, like the dance of a mad peacock.

"My father used to bring me here when I was little."

"And was it always so crowded?"

"Of course," I said. Though I leaned close to him, we had trouble hearing each other. "We waited the whole year for the circus to come—like a village festival."

Long lines had formed in front of the rides. The smells of food drifted over from the stalls. The translator studied each attraction as though it were some exotic sight. My skirt had dried, and I had begun to forget my troubles at the Iris.

"Should we get on one of the rides?"

"You go. I'll wait for you here."

"No, I don't want to go without you. That's no fun. Look, everyone here has someone to be with."

In the end, we rode a little airplane in the shape of Dumbo the elephant. The elephant was sky blue, with trunk held aloft and ears flared out. We climbed in, propping our feet on the ears. Our knees were bent double and our shoulders hunched in order to fit into the tiny seats.

The translator seemed ill at ease, and he tugged continually at his suit, as if afraid it would get wrinkled. A buzzer sounded, the wires creaked, and the elephants lifted into the air. The translator let out a startled gasp.

"Here we go!" I laughed. "You've never been on a ride like this? Never even been to the circus before?"

"No."

"I don't believe it! Why not?"

"No reason, really. I just never had the chance, and I'm not very good with heights." The elephants suddenly started to move forward. I screamed and grasped the guardrail, afraid I would be thrown out. The breeze swirled around us, and my skirt billowed. The wisps of hair on the translator's head stood on end.

There was still light in the sky, but the sun was sinking slowly into the darkness at the horizon. A pale moon rose over the seawall.

The sea looked smaller from above. The island floated peacefully on the waves. The lights from the booths and rides blurred into a single bright mass, and at the center, the band played the same tune over and over.

"Are you all right?" I called over the noise. "Are you having fun?" His eyes were shut tight, but he nodded.

I looked out to where the Iris must have been among the jumble of buildings in the distance, but I couldn't make out the hotel. The whole world was spinning rapidly with us.

He seemed dizzy long after we got off the ride.

"Do you feel bad?" I asked.

"No, I'm fine," he said, running his fingers through his hair. We held hands again and wandered past the other rides.

With dusk the fairground grew crowded. Children called out in excitement and rushed about clutching balloons or cotton candy. Strolling performers spat fire. Startled by the impromptu show, a baby began to cry. Couples wandered along arm in arm, stopping to hug and kiss as if there were no one else about. Popcorn and ticket stubs skittered across the grounds ahead of the breeze. A bottle rocket shot up from somewhere, a stray dog raced through the crowd, flashbulbs popped.

The translator's hand was soft. So soft, it seemed my hand would sink completely into his. This hand had done so many things to me—stroked my hair, made my tea, stripped me, bound me—and with each new act it had been reborn as something different. But was the hand that held mine now the same one that had killed a woman? The thought occurred to me at times, but it did not frighten me in the least. Had this hand strangled her? Or stabbed her with a pair of scissors? Or made her drink poison? I had no idea. But I could easily imagine how gracefully the fingers would have done those things . . . the curve of the knuckles, the faint web of blue veins.

Leaning against the fence of the merry-go-round, we ate ice cream cones. The translator stared for a moment at his cone—chocolate and vanilla swirled together in a spiral.

"It's going to melt if you don't eat it," I warned.

"But it's such a fascinating shape."

"It's just soft ice cream," I told him.

"I almost never eat it."

"You have to do it like this," I said, opening my mouth wide and taking a huge bite. He watched me, and then, holding his cone as if it might break, he bent forward and cautiously licked the very top. A drop melted on his pants, and he hurried to pull out his handkerchief and wipe it away. I took the handkerchief to help him, thinking how much simpler eating ice cream should have been than taking off my clothes and tying me up.

"I always had an ice cream cone when I came here with my father. I could pick one ride and one treat, that was the rule. As we left the house, Mother would remind me, 'Only one, now! Don't forget, and don't go begging for anything more.'"

"But why was she so strict?"

"She thought the fair was a waste of money. That's all she cared about. But Papa always let me have something extra as long as I didn't tell Mother. The best part was wandering

around trying to decide what to choose. A candy apple, or
the shooting gallery, or maybe the haunted house. . . . I felt
as though a genie had offered to grant me a wish. And Papa
would stay right there with me, waiting patiently, no matter
how long I took to decide."

The wooden horses spun on and on behind us, while
Dumbo made his endless flight. The sun set and the sky
turned a deep indigo, but the stars were obscured by the lights
of the fair. A balloon floated up on the breeze and drifted off
toward the sea.

"You love your father, don't you?" said the translator.

"I did," I said, brushing the crumbs of the cone from my
blouse, "but he died when I was eight. He was thirty-one.
Everyone said he was too young."

"I'm sorry, I didn't know." He looked down at the spot on
his pants.

"He was drunk and got into a fight. He hit his head somehow, but we don't know exactly what happened. When they
found him, his body was behind the movie theater. People
talked about it for days, how blood was pouring out of his
nose and ears, how his skull had split open and his brains
were everywhere—all kinds of stories, even though they never
saw him." The translator was trying to finish the last bit of his
cone without getting his hands dirty. He pursed his lips and
nibbled the end of the cone. "But it wasn't really as bad as they
said. It's true, his face was bruised and swollen, but when we
cleaned him up, his eyes were clear and bright, almost as if he

were alive, as though he might suddenly look up and apologize for giving us such a scare."

A buzzer sounded, and the horses on the merry-go-round spun slowly to a stop. The riders emerged reluctantly from the exit as the children who had been waiting impatiently for the next turn ran in to claim the biggest and best horses. Then the buzzer sounded again, the music started, and the horses sprang to life—over and over again. It seemed that nothing would ever interrupt this endless repetition, as though the horses and the children had ridden off into some cul-de-sac of time never to emerge again.

"Mother was convinced someone had attacked him, and she tried everything to find who did it. She wanted to collect damages. But it was useless. There was no trace of him." I paused for a moment and then added, "Have you ever seen a body?"

"What?" he blurted out. He had been wiping his mouth with his handkerchief.

"A dead body."

"You mean a corpse?" he said.

"No, not a 'corpse.' Not someone who lived out his life and died slowly of old age. A *body*! Someone who never saw it coming, who never had a chance. I mean the 'body' of someone who died suddenly, out of the blue."

He slowly refolded the handkerchief in his lap and licked his lips, as if still not convinced he'd managed to wipe away the ice cream.

"I have," he said at last. "A number of times."

"Where?"

"I don't know . . . during the air raids, and someone who committed suicide on the train tracks, and in a traffic accident." He seemed reluctant to answer and sat there pressing on his temples, trying to unravel the thread of an inexplicably tangled thought.

"But I want to know the details."

"Why?"

"Just because," I said. Because I thought his wife's was among those bodies.

"Well, now that you mention it, I did see the body of a child who fell off the excursion boat about ten years ago."

"Really? What was it like?" I moved closer and rested against him. He leaned over slightly to support my head and wrapped his arm around my back. The fence swayed. When I looked up, I saw a tiny patch of stubble that his razor had missed.

"He was a beautiful little boy, about four years old. His skin was very fair, and his hair was naturally curly. He was very well behaved and was sitting with his mother on a bench on the deck. But something must have caught his eye, a seagull diving for fish or someone riding a Jet Ski, and he went running off toward the back of the boat. In the blink of an eye, he leaned over the rail and fell in. There was nothing his mother could have done, it happened so quickly. We all saw him, but it was as though he was being dragged overboard by some sea demon. His body fell in a smooth, even arc and hit the water with a quiet splash." His voice shook as he spoke.

"And then?" I breathed the question into his neck.

"Strictly speaking, I never saw the body. Just the boy bobbing on the waves and then sinking under them. He didn't seem to be suffering terribly. In fact, he seemed puzzled, as though he were wondering how he had come to be in such a predicament. His mother called his name, and the other passengers gathered along the rail. Someone tossed him a life preserver, but a big wave washed over him and he was gone."

"Did they ever find the body?"

"No." He shook his head, and I felt his every tremor through my cheek as I leaned against his shoulder. Coming through his bones, his voice sounded clearer and calmer, as though it were welling up from the depths.

Someone dropped a cup of soda in the dirt. There was a burst of laughter, drowned out almost immediately by the band. The flags and the leaves and the lights of the stalls swayed in the cool evening breeze.

It wouldn't have taken long for the fish to clean everything away, and now his bones glowed faintly at the bottom of the sea, the two empty eyeholes staring up at the translator and me as we made our way to the island.

"Even here, I feel as though we're the only two people in the world," I said.

"We're always alone. We need no one else." He stroked my hair, which was limp with perspiration but still pinned up in Mother's neat bun, while his other hand worked busily at the spot on his pants. His efforts had only made the stain worse, and I began to worry that the material would give way under his rubbing.

The fire-eater blew a stream of flame into the air. A donkey with a child on its back ambled past. The crescent moon, which had been white a moment before, glowed orange.

EIGHT

It was a hot summer, the hottest I had known. Venturing outside during the day, even for a short while, made me dizzy from the heat. The light was so dazzling that the shoreline and even the sea took on a yellowish cast. There were many cases of sunstroke down at beach, and the sirens of the ambulances could be heard at the Iris.

The guests used the showers in their rooms to cool off, and there was water running somewhere at every hour. The plants in the courtyard wilted in the heat, but the cicadas clinging to the zelkova tree sang day and night. Cracks had begun to form on the boy in the fountain.

According to the radio forecast, the heat wave had no end in sight. Our guests muttered about the weather around the breakfast table in hushed, tired voices, but they went off to the beach just the same. An open container of yogurt left out overnight went sour overnight. Mother and the maid used the heat as an excuse to drink beer all day, and they went about their chores with red cheeks. The heat lingered into the evening, long after the sun set, and there was no sign of rain or even a breeze. It seemed as though summer would go on forever, as though the seasons had stopped changing.

One day, he ordered me to put his socks on for him. "But you can't use your hands," he said. Unsure exactly what he meant, I looked around the room in confusion, mopping the sweat from my face. "Only your mouth." I quickly put my arms behind my back, understanding for the first time how much trouble hands could be.

I was terribly afraid—not that he would hurt me but that I might not please him. Would I end up being useless to him? Would I forfeit the love he had expressed in his letters because I couldn't obey his orders? Fear welled up in me.

"You have no hands," he said, then suddenly, lifting his leg with perfect grace and confidence, he delivered a smooth, sharp kick to the back. I lost balance and fell to my knees.

On the island, he could do what he wanted with my body, and my soul. "Wipe the sweat off your face," he said. "Lick it." As he spoke, he prodded my bare breasts with the tips of his fingers.

My clothes were wadded in a ball under the desk. On top, as always, the tools of the translator's trade were neatly laid out. The novel about Marie, the dictionaries, and the notebook. I had no idea whether he'd made any progress on the translation. It seemed as though more pages of the book had been turned, but the page in the notebook always looked the same.

He had undressed me with great skill, his movements no less elegant for all their violence. Indeed, the more he shamed me, the more refined he became—like a perfumer plucking the petals from a rose, a jeweler prying open an oyster for its pearl.

I stuck out my tongue to lick the sweat from my lips, forcing it out as far as I could until I nearly choked. Then I wiped the places I couldn't reach on the rug. It was scratchy and burned my skin. My back ached where he had kicked me.

"That's right," he said. He looked larger, seen from below like this, as though his shoulders and chest had suddenly become broad and strong. But the skin was still slack on his neck, and the wrinkles creased when he spoke. "Now the socks, and be quick about it."

I crawled to the bedroom and then struggled to my feet. But as I was about to open the wardrobe, I was kicked once again.

"How many times do I have to tell you? No hands!"

I was disgusted with myself. How could I make the same mistake? He had been so clear. I had no hands!

I took the knob on the wardrobe in my mouth. It was hard and rough and had a strange taste. No matter how hard I pulled, I couldn't open it. He was watching me from behind, arms crossed, his eyes piercing my back, studying every detail.

He knew much more than I did about my skin—the delicate curves and hollows and clefts, the positions of the moles.

At last the hinges creaked and the door opened. The smell of mothballs filled the room. It was almost empty inside—three suits, a coat, and four neckties—and everything was perfectly pressed, hung at precisely spaced intervals. One of the suits—the one he had stained at the fair, I realized—was still in the cleaner's plastic bag.

I looked for socks, but there were none, even in the dark recesses at the back. So I tried the little drawers inside the wardrobe, opening them one after another with my teeth. Without my hands, this body was weak and useless . . . clumsy, pathetic, disgraceful.

I found tiepins and sport shirts and handkerchiefs, all permeated with the smell of mothballs, but no socks. I was getting anxious. Pushing back the handkerchiefs, I used my chin to look under the shirts. I was afraid of disturbing his perfectly ordered drawer but even more afraid of failing to fulfill his demands. He made no move to help me or to excuse my pitiful efforts.

The world outside was bathed in summer sunlight. The curtains hung limp by the window. Half the lawn had turned brown from the heat, and the terrace was sharply divided, half in light and half in shadow. We were alone, and the world was silent; not the trill of a cicada or even the sound of the waves reached us here.

At last I came to the smallest drawer at the bottom of the wardrobe. By getting down on my stomach and extending my neck, I managed to open it. Inside, I found a pocket watch, a wristwatch, cuff links, a case for eyeglasses—and in the very back, something odd: a woman's scarf.

It was pale pink silk with a floral pattern, and of all the things I had discovered in the wardrobe, it was clearly the only one that did not belong. But not simply because it was a woman's scarf. Something else had caught my attention, and I tried to pull it out to get a better look. The scarf was covered with dark spots, and the edges were badly tattered. I was sure the spots were blood.

"Not that!" he cried, ripping the scarf from my mouth as I raised my head in surprise. He pulled so violently that my lips burned. "Why don't you listen to me? I said I wanted socks!"

Then he hit me. Dropping to one knee, he slapped me again and again across the face. The dry sound echoed in the silence. Warm liquid spread across my tongue, filling my mouth and spilling from between my lips. I didn't know that blood was so warm and soft.

"You're constantly sticking your nose in things that don't concern you. You're a filthy pig, a worthless bitch." His voice was shaking with rage, and he was losing control of himself. He seemed to be dissolving into a formless fury, as he had when they'd turned us away from the restaurant. His knees, his lips, the tips of his fingers—everything seemed to tremble. The veins were throbbing at his temples. He was warping, breaking up, and from the fissures poured endless rage.

"I'm sorry. I didn't know it was so important. I just

wondered what it was and I wanted to get a better look. I won't do it again. Please forgive me, I beg you."

"Do you want to see what I do when you don't obey me?" He kicked me in the side, sending me sprawling on my back, and then he quickly wrapped the scarf around my neck. "I'll show you," he said. "I will."

Then he choked me. The scarf tightened around my throat, compressing bone and muscle and flesh with a sound like fabric slowly tearing. I couldn't breath, couldn't beg him for mercy. My legs thrashed, and I grabbed his wrist, trying unsuccessfully to loosen the scarf.

I couldn't see his face, but I could tell that he was furious by the force of his hands behind my neck, by his groans, by the heat of his breath on my hair. I was trying to submit, but he pulled all the tighter.

"It's your fault," he repeated again and again, as if uttering a curse. "Why do you resist? Why don't you listen?" But then his voice faded and the silence in the room grew heavy and deep. I caught a glimpse of the sea outside the window, but it seemed terribly far away, somewhere beyond the sky. The pain behind my eyes faded slowly to a throbbing burn, and as it did my fear of suffocation vanished. I was being strangled, but oddly I felt that he was crushing my eyes in his hands.

He had wrapped my beautiful eyes in this tattered old scarf and knotted the ends over and over to make sure they wouldn't fall out. When he was done, he took them in his hands and began to gently squeeze them. As he did, I could feel the membranes rupturing, the lenses splitting, liquid spilling out. The heat of my body soaked into the scarf. Finally, my eyes dissolved with a whispering sound. There was a new stain on the scarf.

Colors began to fade. Shadows spread, as if we were sinking to the bottom of the sea, and at some point I realized that pain had been replaced by a cool shadow settling over my body. I wanted to stay wrapped in this shadow forever.

The eyes of the boy who had fallen from the boat appeared before me, and though I had lost my own eyes, I could see them clearly. I wondered for the first time then whether I was going to die. I was certain that the translator's wife had died just like this.

When I woke up, the scarf had been unknotted and slipped from my neck. It lay on the floor near my face, just a tattered square of cloth, stained and stretched out of shape, brightened only by the tiny splashes of blood that had dripped from my mouth. I tried to take a deep breath and fell into a coughing fit. I rubbed my throat, then blinked my eyes to be sure they were unharmed.

The translator was sprawled on the bed, out of breath. His hair was damp with sweat, and patches of scalp were showing through. His anger had apparently vanished, though I had no idea why.

"Now," he said, taking my face in his hands, "the socks."

At last I located the socks in a drawer next to the one that held the scarf. The heels were worn, and the elastic was limp, and they smelled like dried mushrooms.

I had never seen his feet before, or for that matter any bare part of his body. My heart beat faster at the thought that my lips were going to touch him in such a place.

"What a lovely, clever mouth." He sat down on the edge of the bed and crossed his legs. Kneeling in front of him, I brought my head to his foot and began to pull the sock over his toes. It wasn't easy. The shape of a foot is more complicated than I had imagined, and the sock was limp and difficult to hold in my mouth.

"Now the other one," he said, crossing his legs the other way. At some point he must have smoothed his hair and covered the bald patches.

His feet were very clean—the nails neatly clipped, smelling faintly of soap—but they were old. The skin was pale and dry, and the heels were cracked. The nails on the little toes had been deformed by long years in hard leather shoes. Blue veins covered the tops of the feet, and the skin on the ankles was rough. The hair on his toes tickled my cheek. I licked them gently, hoping he might not notice, thrilled to be kissing him.

My moist lips caressed his weathered feet. Their color, dyed deeper than usual by the blood from my mouth, showed bright against his pale skin. I used only my lips. He sat on the edge of the bed, dressed in his suit, and I knelt on the floor, completely naked—and yet I had the sense that we were lost in each other's arms. I kissed every inch, and as I

did, I felt that my mouth was lovely and clever, just as he had
said.

. . . *The boat is always full now. Unless you're lucky, there is rarely
a place to sit or even space to lean against the rail on deck. The tourists stand chatting, arms and legs bared to the sun. I try to be incon-
spicuous, finding a seat on one of the small benches next to the
stairway. They're not very popular because they are far from the
windows and the best views of the sea. From time to time, some
thoughtless traveler will leave his bag on one of the benches, but I toss
it on the floor and take the seat.*

*They all seem to be at pains to avoid making eye contact with
me, as if I weren't even there. But that suits me well enough. I like
to think about you on the boat. Not one person in that huge crowd
knows what you did to my feet. Nor do they know that your left
breast is slightly larger than your right, that you have a habit of
touching your earlobe when you're frightened, or that you have a
dimple on your thigh. Or how lovely your pale face looks when you
are on the verge of suffocating and want to ask for my help. I am the
only one who knows everything about you. I pore over my secrets
there on the boat, and savor their various pleasures.*

*How long will this heat continue? It's the worst hot spell I have seen
since moving to the island, and I am longing for winter. I imagine how
nice it will be to walk through the cold, deserted town with you, once
the summer has ended and the tourists have gone. Though one thing
does bother me: the last boat of the day leaves an hour earlier in winter.
I hope you don't find me ridiculous for worrying about such things.*

It happens every year that demand for my translation services drops off sharply in the summer. I haven't had anything like a real job for some time now. But then translating from Russian has never been a profitable line of work. I suppose the number of people in this world who find themselves inconvenienced because they don't understand Russian is really rather small.

Two or three years ago, I decided to try teaching Russian. I took some money from my savings, and I placed an advertisement in the newspaper. "Study Russian! Conversation, translation. Beginners welcome." After the advertisement appeared, I waited every day for some response. But not one person answered the ad. Around the time the boat was due in, I would go out and stand on the porch. I listened for footsteps on the road down by the cove, but it was pointless. No one ever came climbing up the shell stairs. I had wasted my money.

But since I met you I have learned the real meaning of waiting. I have experienced the indescribable joy of waiting for you, there in front of the flower clock in the plaza, and I am inordinately happy, even before you appear to me.

I watch the people coming up from the shore road, staring at every girl with even the slightest resemblance to you, and then turning away when I realize my mistake. I perform this ritual over and over, never growing tired. I would gladly repeat my error a thousand times, two thousand times, if it means finding you, you who are wholly unique. Finally, I am at a loss to distinguish between the desire to see you as soon as possible and the pleasant prospect of waiting forever.

On the day we went to the circus, I had the great joy of waiting for three hours and twenty minutes. And still today, I find myself dreaming of you as you came running up to me that day, perspiring profusely, with the setting sun shining at your back.

When the longing to see you becomes more than I can bear, I find solace in Marie. I translate line after line, writing them out in my notebook, and it calms me a bit to turn the pages and watch them fill up with her story.

Marie's parents are opposed to her affair with the riding master and they shut her up in a lakeside villa and force her to marry a barrister. The riding master is conscripted into the military and sent far away. One day, Marie realizes that she is pregnant. When her husband finds out, he strips her naked, plunges her into the frigid lake, and then forces her to take a medicine to induce miscarriage.

It's a splendid scene. When Marie has been stripped in the forest at the edge of the lake, her corset and garters and brassiere hang from the branches of the birch trees like exotic white flowers. She resists, but he seizes her by the hair and throws her into the lake. Her golden locks spread out on the surface, and the green water dyes her translucent skin. She does not know how to swim, so her arms and legs thrash uselessly and her mouth opens and closes in wild convulsions. The barrister forces the medicine down her throat, and when Marie gulps for air, she swallows the potion. . . .

I can picture every detail of Marie's suffering, from the way the seaweed wraps about her ankles to the echoes of her cries among the birches. And then, in my mind, you, Mari, have taken her place.

Would you like to have lunch at my home next Tuesday? I will cook for you. Thanks to these long years of living alone, I have a degree of confidence in the kitchen. This is an excellent idea, I think, and I feel certain that the meal will surprise you. I am already full of anticipation.

Come at eleven, or at noon, at any hour that suits you. I'll wait for you at home. Please make your escape from the Iris. I implore you.

I hope you manage to avoid the worst of the heat. Take care of yourself.

Until we meet again, my dear Mari.

It was certainly no ordinary lunch. I realized that things were different as soon as I walked in the door. There was a subtle change in the atmosphere of the house, and while it wasn't unpleasant, I sensed that things could never go back to the way they had been.

A pot was boiling on the stove, and a striped blue cloth covered the table. Two hibiscus flowers were floating in a glass bowl, and dishes of food crowded every remaining space. A radio sat on the serving cart next to the drinks, playing a classical piece I did not know.

Where had he found the flowers? This was not a house for charming decorations. And the music? Other than the accordion tunes played by the boy in the plaza, we had never listened to music of any sort when we were together.

But I was most shocked to find that the translator was not alone.

"I'm so glad you could come," he said. "It must have been hot on the boat. Please come in. Did you manage to find an excuse to get away? And can you spend the afternoon with us? Let me get you something cold to drink." He was clearly in high spirits and couldn't stop talking. He had taken off his suit jacket and loosened his tie, and he had even removed his cuff links and rolled up his sleeves. "But first I should introduce you—this is my nephew. He'll be staying with me for a week."

The young man stood and bowed to me without looking up.

"Hello," I said, still quite confused. He sat down again and crossed his legs, settling deep into the couch. He was tall and thin, and his curly hair was long enough to cover his ears. He wore tight black pants and a white T-shirt, but around his neck was an oddly shaped pendant that was out of keeping with his simple clothes. It was the only thing remarkable about his appearance. It might have been a piece of art, or a charm or talisman.

A silence fell in the room. The translator's nephew said nothing, ignoring the usual niceties. A piano solo began on the radio; the lid on the pot started to rattle.

"Aah," said the translator, "I should have mentioned it right away. He was sick at one point, and ever since he has been unable to talk."

"He can't talk?"

"That's right. But it's nothing to worry about. He just won't be able to answer you. . . . I'd better see to lunch. It will be ready soon, just have a seat."

I felt ill at ease after he went into the kitchen. What did one do with a person who couldn't talk? And besides, I was having difficulty accepting that someone other than the translator was sitting on the couch. Did this young man, with his slender hips and comfortably crossed legs, know what sorts of humiliating things had been done to me on that couch? The thought made me more and more uncomfortable.

He motioned for me to sit down, but he still avoided looking at me. When our eyes met, he looked away immediately, focusing on some random point, a scratch on the coffee table, a frayed patch on a cushion, or the tips of his fingers. Then he would keep his head down, staring, for some time, as though he had always wanted to examine that particular spot.

I sat across from him. We could hear the translator bustling about in the kitchen, and then the sound of the piano on the radio. Eventually, the woodwinds joined in.

Suddenly, a slip of paper was in my hand. *"It's Chopin,"* the note said. *"His First Concerto. Do you know it?"*

The pendant around his neck was in fact a thin, silver-plated case, like one you might use for cigarettes, except his held a small notepad. He had opened it, torn off a page, written the note with a tiny pen, and slipped it into my hand without a sound.

"I've never heard it before," I said.

"It's wonderful, don't you think?"

"I do. I love it." In fact, I was much more interested in our strange conversation, and I had hardly heard the music, but I was anxious to agree with him.

The click of the case as he popped it open; the sparkling white of the paper; the tip of the pen as it traced the characters; the casual way he passed me the note—it was almost like he had a voice.

Then he put away the pen and closed the lid of the case. I coughed quietly and drew a meaningless pattern on the carpet with the toe of my shoe. We fell silent again. The sound of the waves seemed closer than usual.

He stood up abruptly and went into the kitchen to adjust the radio. It was clearly a very old model, and though it was large and impressive, the sound was poor. The antenna was rusted and one of the knobs was missing, but eventually he managed to improve the reception.

Apparently, he had visited his uncle here more than once in the past, and he didn't seem the least bit affected by the obsessive orderliness in the house. Whether he was opening a door or adjusting the radio, his manner was utterly natural, as if he had been doing it just that way for many years.

I, on the other hand, felt as though I was seeing the house for the first time and realizing that there were aspects of the translator's life he'd kept hidden from me—to begin with, the fact that he owned a radio. He hadn't kept it in the wardrobe, that much was certain. Perhaps he'd had it in the drawer of his desk? Or in the back of the dish cupboard? But why had the radio—not to mention the flowers—suddenly appeared on the occasion of his nephew's visit? Why for him and not for me? Questions came to me one after the other, like the sound of the surf.

"We're ready at last! You must be famished. We'll eat here in the kitchen." The translator was oblivious to all my questions. "Would you show her where to sit?"

Those were the first words he had addressed to his nephew since I'd arrived, a simple, harmless request.

The nephew obediently pulled out my chair and signaled that I should be seated. I crumpled up the two notes he had given me and slipped them in my pocket.

When I first saw the dishes on the table, I had trouble believing that it was all for us to eat. I wondered, in fact, whether the display wasn't simply another part of the translator's new décor, like the hibiscus or the Chopin concerto.

There was no solid food. Everything was pulped or mashed or liquefied, as if for a baby just being weaned. There were no knives or forks at our places, only spoons. We didn't need anything else.

But these soups and liquids were all beautiful colors. A deep green, slightly gritty mixture in the salad bowls that tasted of spinach and butter. Blood red in the soup bowls that I immediately identified as tomato, but with a complicated blend of spices. And on the large dinner plates, pools of bright yellow. It looked so much like paint that I hesitated before taking the first bite. My spoon made little eddies on the surface and released a puff of steam. I couldn't imagine what it was or how he'd made it. It smelled like a cross between damp leaves on the forest floor and washed-up seaweed.

"Do you come here every year?" I asked.

"No, not necessarily," the translator replied for him. "I think it's been three years since he was here. He's quite busy, even during the summer holidays. He's been doing study tours for his seminar, assisting one of his professors, and working on his thesis."

"What is he studying?"

"Architecture. He's an expert on the Gothic style. From the time he was a small child, he loved buildings. He used to make houses out of blocks for hours on end, but always the most unusual designs, the sort of thing no adult could imagine. And then at some point he started buying postcards of medieval churches, and he put together a remarkable collection—all churches, mind you. I doubt there are too many children in the world who show this kind of taste. With boys, it's usually cars or baseball players or comic books. He was a strange child, to say the least." As he finished speaking, the translator wiped his mouth with his napkin and then stirred the contents of his bowl with a spoon.

"And what does he plan to do when he graduates?"

"Continue his studies at a research center." The nephew reached for his pendant, but the translator stopped him. "No, don't bother. You should enjoy your lunch in peace. If you start writing, you can't eat. We can talk as much as we want and eat at the same time," he said, though he was the only one actually talking.

"What is the Gothic style?" I asked, wondering what would happen if I asked a question the translator could not answer.

"He can show you his postcards later," the translator said before his nephew could begin to write. "And he has sketches from his travels. He's a brilliant artist, too. He comes here to have time to draw."

His nephew continued to spoon up his lunch, apparently content to let his uncle answer for him. Though we were talking about him, he barely acknowledged us and simply went on quietly eating. From time to time, the pendant knocked softly against the edge of the table.

The only easily identifiable item on the table was the water. I asked for more, and the translator filled my glass from the pitcher on the serving cart. The music stopped for a moment and I thought the concerto had ended, but then it started again, apparently beginning another movement.

"Do you like it?" the translator asked.

"Yes," I murmured noncommittally. "It's quite unusual."

"I went to the market yesterday and started preparing last night. It's been a long time since I've spent the day cooking." He seemed quite proud of himself.

"But do you always cook everything until it turns to soup?" I asked, trying not to sound critical.

"Yes, when my nephew is here." The two of them exchanged a glance, some sign known only to them, and I realized I would never get used to the idea of anyone coming between us, of him trading looks with someone other than me.

I felt as though the three of us were on a crazy Ferris wheel—as I braced on one corner of the seat, holding my breath, the nephew sunk in silence on the other side, and only the translator, in the middle, seemed to enjoy himself. And the more pleasure he took, the more violently the seat seemed to rock.

"I usually cook for him myself. When he writes to say he's coming, the first thing I do is get out the blender. We go out sometimes, too, but he can't order anything but soup, or thin stew."

"Why is that?"

"Because he has no tongue." The ice rattled in his glass. His nephew pushed back an empty plate and pulled another one nearer. I counted the yellow drops falling from my spoon as I let the meaning of his words sink in. "When he was a child, he developed a malignant tumor on his tongue. So they had to remove it."

"I don't believe you," I said.

"But it's true. Sad, but true." He said nothing more on the subject.

I glanced as discreetly as possible at his mouth, hoping neither of them would notice. From the outside, everything seemed normal. His lips were perfectly formed, and each spoonful of food seemed to run smoothly down his throat. I felt a sudden wave of panic. Did I have a tongue of my own? I bit down softly to be sure.

The translator went on talking, barely taking a breath between stories of his nephew's exploits. He bragged about his achievements and boasted about his future prospects. He told how he'd been born half dead, with his umbilical cord wrapped around his neck. How he had appeared as a baby in a commercial for powdered milk. How he'd got lost in a department store. How he'd saved a kitten from drowning in a river and been written up in the newspaper. The stories came bubbling out of him like baby spiders hatching from their eggs, each episode giving rise to another memory, anecdote, or tirade against an imagined enemy.

The only figure who failed to appear anywhere in all of this talk was the translator's dead wife, the woman who had been strangled with the scarf. She had completely vanished.

I was barely listening; it took all my energy to keep the boredom from showing on my face. The nephew, on the other hand, sat there eating his meal, apparently unfazed by the translator's endless soliloquy—so much so that I began to wonder whether they had also removed his eardrums.

But the translator did not seem to care whether we were listening. He simply went on hatching baby spiders into the void in front of him, apparently unable to stop until there were no more.

I put down my spoon, having managed to eat only half of what had been set in front of me. I didn't want to disappoint him, but I had begun to feel sick, and my skirt was glued to my thighs with perspiration. I was worried he would dissolve in anger because I rejected his cooking, that his brain and organs and bones and fat would come apart. I wondered

whether his nephew would know any better than I did how
to put him back together again.

Then I suddenly realized he had stopped talking. The last
egg had hatched. He tipped up his plate and was noisily
spooning up the dregs of a dark red paste. Applause crackled
from the radio; it was the end of the concerto.

"You don't look much alike," I said, thinking this might
bring the conversation around to the subject of his wife. But
he said nothing. He was as intent now on finishing his meal
as he had been on the conversation a moment before.

"Because we're not related by blood," the nephew answered at
last. He could write with amazing speed even on such a
crowded table, and his movements seemed all the more discreet after the translator's long soliloquy. *"My uncle's wife and
my mother were sisters."* The note slid noiselessly across the table.

"He told me that his wife died," I said. I was curious how
the translator would react if I spoke directly to his nephew.
The young man tore out another sheet of paper and began
writing a longer note with his small pen.

"Does anyone have room for dessert?" asked the translator.
"We have peach sorbet and banana mousse. They're in the
refrigerator. But first, we should clear the table a bit. Could
you give me a hand?" His nephew put the note he'd been
writing back in the case and stood up to help.

Their efforts were remarkably efficient, as if they had
agreed on the division of labor ahead of time. A glance or
slight gesture was enough for them to understand one another, and there was nothing left for me to do.

The hibiscus flowers were so fresh they seemed to sparkle. It was as hot as ever outside, but from time to time a breeze passed through the window above the kitchen sink and out across the terrace to the south. Each time it did, the pages of Marie's novel fluttered quietly. A new piece started to play on the radio; I had no idea what it was.

They served the sorbet and the mousse. I wondered what the nephew had been writing in his note and how he could get along so well with a man who had killed his aunt. There were many things I didn't understand. The mousse melted and slid down my throat.

The translator strangled me over and over in my dreams, always with the same scarf. I learned every stain and frayed edge by heart.

The pain would build until it became unbearable, and just when I thought I couldn't stand it anymore, when I felt I was sinking to the bottom of the sea, the nephew would appear out of nowhere.

"Because we're not related by blood," he would write quickly on his notepad, and the translator would immediately stop strangling me and turn his attention to finding something by Chopin on the radio. Then he would tie the scarf around his nephew's neck. Though it was a woman's scarf, it suited him perfectly and was a good match for his pendant. . . .

———

I had nearly suffocated once before, long ago. My father was still alive, so I must have been in first or second grade.

At the time, I was strictly forbidden from going into the guest rooms, and Mother told me the story of our resident ghost to discourage me.

"Many years ago, she committed suicide here with her lover," Mother told me, though I was too young to know what "suicide" meant. "She doesn't bother customers, only naughty little girls. She rips them open with her long finger-nails and eats their insides."

Needless to say, I stayed out of the guest rooms—except once.

I don't remember why, but one morning I absolutely could not bring myself to go to school, and so I pretended to leave the hotel but then crept back and hid in Room 301. I was planning to reappear in the afternoon when I would normally arrive home from school.

I passed the time reading comic books on the bed and eating the chocolate I'd hidden in my backpack, though I was careful not to make a sound or leave a single crumb behind. From time to time I'd hear Mother's voice somewhere nearby and nearly die of fright, but I was also thrilled by the danger.

There was just one flaw in my plan: at around noon, some guests checked in to the room. There had been no reservations for that day—I knew because my grandfather had taught me how to decipher the guest book and I had checked to be sure that 301 was free. Nonetheless, a couple walked through the door just a half hour before school would have been ending.

I grabbed my backpack and dove into the closet. As I did, I hit my elbow hard on the corner of the dresser, but I pressed my hand over my mouth to keep from crying out. The closet door was slightly ajar, and when I peeked out I could see a young woman and a middle-aged man.

They had barely set down their luggage when they started to argue. The woman did most of the talking, telling the man he was worthless and thoughtless and stuck-up, and then calling him every bad name she could think of. Meanwhile, the man just muttered quietly and punched the bed with his fist.

Suddenly, I realized that I'd forgotten my shoes. They were lined up neatly by the bed, with the toes tucked under the comforter. What would I do if they found them? A pair of little girl's shoes was sure to strike them as strange, and they were bound to tell Mother.

My chest began to ache. My heart was beating fast, and I broke out in a cold sweat. I probably should have been worried about one of them opening the closet, but for some reason, at the time, I was obsessed with the shoes.

The woman walked right by them several times, almost stepping on them. Why had I remembered my backpack but completely forgotten about the shoes? Why had I taken them off in the first place? Why had I been so worried about getting the quilt dirty?

Liar! Worthless good-for-nothing! Coward! We're through! It's all your fault. I always knew you were a bastard, a bum! . . . Her threats and insults were getting more violent. But I was terrified that the man would explode, that he would kill her.

Then I remembered my mother's story, and I felt as though the long-nailed ghost was standing right outside the closet door. I started having trouble breathing, as if I'd used up all the air in the closet. I was terrified that the ghost would pull me out and slice open my belly with her fingernail, and I could feel a scream building in my throat. As long as they were there in the room, I couldn't get away. I couldn't even cry out for help. I might have to spend all night in this dark box. I was so terrified, I fainted.

That was the first time I felt the pain of being unable to breathe, but at the moment I lost consciousness, I felt wonderful, as though my body was being absorbed into the sea—the same feeling I'd had years later when the translator strangled me with the scarf.

When I came to, there was a crowd around me. My father was holding me in his arms, and my grandfather was peering at me over his shoulder. My mother was apologizing to the couple, who were no longer fighting. My father made me take a sip of whiskey from the flask he kept in his back pocket. That was the one and only time that his alcohol served a useful purpose.

One day, I went swimming with the translator and his nephew. I hadn't known the translator could swim and wouldn't have even imagined he owned a bathing suit.

We rented an umbrella on the beach, at the edge of the crowd. There was a haze on the horizon and the surf was high, but the heat was still oppressive. Some shorebirds floated on the breeze. The island was a blur in the distance.

The translator rubbed coconut suntan oil on his nephew, moving his hands gently from his neck to his back, from his chest to the tips of his fingers. The nephew's young skin quickly absorbed the sickly sweet oil. The pendant hung on his bare chest, and when the translator brushed it with his palm, there was a flash of silver. The nephew was much more muscular than I had imagined, with a strong chest and powerful arms and legs. His body was well formed in every respect—the line from his shoulders to his hips, the alignment of his chest and arms, his smooth, sand-colored skin. It seemed odd that he was so fit, eating nothing but liquid foods.

The translator's hands worked over his body. Just as my mouth had with his feet. Eagerly. Earnestly.

"Now it's your turn, Mari," he said at last.

"No," I told him. "I don't like the smell of the oil." But in fact, I didn't want to be touched by the same hands that had touched his nephew.

The two of them went swimming while I stayed under the umbrella to watch our belongings. The nephew took off his pendant. *Could you look after this for me?* he seemed to say as he placed it in my hand.

Children cried out as they chased after the surf. A lost inner tube was floating out to sea. The sand was washed smooth by each wave, only to be pocked with footprints again a moment later.

The tide was out, and the seawall was half exposed, a jagged edge against the calm surface of the sea. Some children had scrambled up to the highest point and were jumping into the water one after the other. White spray billowed up each time one of them hit the surface, but I was too far away to hear the splash. The shorebirds, as if imitating the children, plunged into the sea in search of fish.

A boy wove his way through the umbrellas, selling drinks from a cooler. The family next to us was eating snow cones from paper cups, the mounds of ice dripping brightly colored syrups.

Though the translator and his nephew had disappeared into the crowd as soon as they left our umbrella, it was easy to find them again in the water. They were beyond the breaking waves, swimming out to sea, the nephew cutting through the water with a smooth, powerful crawl stroke while the translator splashed awkwardly along.

With his head exposed just above the water, he propelled forward with a jerk of his arms and legs, churning the sea around himself. Frowning with disapproval as they paddled away, the other swimmers kept their distance. When the translator noticed that he was losing ground on his nephew, he thrashed more frantically to keep from being left behind.

My heart had pounded at the mere sight of his bare feet when we were alone. But now, seeing him in his old, faded bathing suit, I felt only sadness. But it wasn't because his skin was pale or his muscles soft—it was because these things were no longer mine alone. If his nephew would have left us, I would have been happy to rub oil on the translator's body.

"You have no hands! Use your tongue," he might have commanded. Of course, his nephew could never obey that order—he had no tongue.

I wondered how coconut oil tasted. I hoped it wasn't so sweet it numbed the mouth. After all, I wanted to taste every inch of his naked flesh. I would wriggle my tongue into the wrinkles on his belly and lick the blotchy skin on his back, and down along his thighs, to the sandy soles of his feet, spreading the oil everywhere my tongue could reach.

But I wanted this body I worshiped to be ugly—only then could I taste my disgrace. Only when I was brutalized, reduced to a sack of flesh, could I know pure pleasure.

In the end, I regretted having come. I wanted to see the translator alone, and the mere presence of his nephew made me miserable.

The nephew had reached the floats at the edge of the bathing area. He held on to a blue buoy to rest. Meanwhile, the translator was still thrashing, barely halfway out. The lifeguard was watching him through binoculars from the stand on the beach, and I started to worry that he would think the translator was drowning.

I opened the note case on the pendant the nephew had left with me. It seemed larger here in my hand than it had dangling around his neck. The silver plating was marred in places, but with a little click it had quite easily opened, and inside I found a small pad of notepapers, enough to hold all his thoughts.

"Are you alone?" someone said. I looked up to find two boys standing in front of me. They were so much alike they could have been twins. "Would you like to go swimming?" one said. I shook my head. "We'll take you out on our boat. It's in the harbor around the cape."

"And if you don't like boats, we could go dancing tonight. Where are you staying? We're at the Dolphin, the hotel across from the pier. Do you know it?"

The translator had finally reached the buoy, and he and his nephew were clutching the line that secured it, bobbing in the waves.

"Don't be so stuck-up," one of the boys said as he tried to put his hand on my shoulder. I quickly tore a note from the pad, scribbled on it, and handed it to him.

"I can't speak."

They looked at one another and shrugged, then left without another word. The pen had felt good in my hand, and the blue ink flowed smoothly on the paper.

A huge wave broke on the beach, scattering the bathers for a moment. It washed up new shells and driftwood and bits of fishing net. A crab made its way painstakingly across a beach towel. The tide was covering the seawall again.

I suddenly realized that they were waving at me from the surf. I raised my hand to wave back, but then decided not to. Perhaps the sun had been playing tricks on my eyes and no one had waved at all.

———

"You should have come in," said the translator, drying himself with a towel. "It was wonderful."

"I will next time," I said.

"It's colder than I thought it would be. I wonder how far we swam—half a kilometer? It's been a long time since I've been in the water. I usually don't swim unless he's visiting."

He was still in high spirits, but he looked even older than usual when wet. His hair was plastered on his scalp like strands of seaweed, and his bathing suit drooped pathetically. Perhaps he knew how he looked, because he took great care in drying himself.

His nephew retrieved the pendant from me and hung it carefully back around his neck, as if it were very precious. I didn't tell him that I had used a sheet of paper. He was still panting. His breath was cool and smelled of the sea.

The sun had shifted, lengthening the shadow of the umbrella. The nephew brushed his hair from his eyes and lay down, oblivious to the sand on his back. We bought three bottles of soda from the drinks vendor. As the nephew drank, the liquid gurgled down his throat, and for a moment I thought I heard nonsense words in the sound of him swallowing.

"I wonder what people think of us," I said.

"*I suppose they think we're brother and sister, out for a day at the beach with our butler.*" Even lying on his side, he could write quite quickly.

The translator glanced at the note and said, "What a delightful idea. You lost your parents at a young age. You attend separate boarding schools and are only together for vacations. During the summer, you come to your house by the sea. And I am your guardian. A faithful servant who obeys even your most unreasonable orders, who gladly subjects himself to the worst indignities on your behalf, who has sworn his unconditional loyalty to you." He nodded to himself in satisfaction at this scenario and then finished his soda.

"I doubt anyone could guess the truth," I said.

I could see the twins who had approached me earlier talking to another girl. More umbrellas had sprung up, and the sea was full of bobbing heads, some all the way down at the base of the cape.

"It's much more fun if they don't." The translator buried his empty bottle in the sand.

"What shall we do for lunch?" The nephew handed this note to his uncle.

"Are you hungry already?" the translator asked. His nephew nodded his head. "Don't worry, I've got everything prepared at the house. Pureed sea bass and broccoli soup. Your favorites." He put his nephew's sandals next to the blanket, brushed the sand from his shoulders, and straightened the chain on the pendant. Just as a real servant might. "Mari, you'll come, too, won't you?" he said, turning to me with a gentle smile, as if to say he hadn't forgotten me.

"I'm afraid I can't. Mother is expecting me back by noon." I handed him my half-empty soda bottle and went in for a swim. Floating on my back, I let my hair spread out on the surface of the water.

I wanted to be Marie. I wanted him to grab my hair and pull me down to the bottom of the sea, to force me to swallow his bitter potion.

Mother was furious that I had spoiled my hair. "Haven't I told you not to go swimming? Now go get the hair dryer and the brush and the camellia oil, and hurry up! We have too much to do today for you to be dawdling about." In the twinkling of an eye, she had repaired my hair.

Later, when I went out that evening to bring in the wash, my bathing suit was gone. There was no sign of it anywhere. The maid was stealing from me again.

The maid had worked all day, even staying late. She had waxed the floor in the lobby, cut the grass in the courtyard, and washed the windows in the dining room—all while she asked me disturbing questions.

"What would you do if your mother told you she was getting married again?"

"If she leaves you the hotel, would you keep me on?"

"Did you know I was your father's first lover?"

"Are you still seeing that boy?"

I answered halfheartedly or pretended not to hear, but she kept after me just the same. She was probably secretly gloating at having made off with my bathing suit. When Mother handed her a can of beer as she was getting ready to leave, she slipped it into her bag—the bag where she must have hidden my suit.

The next day something odd happened at the beach. Thousands of dead fish washed up on the tide. The news spread through town at dawn, and by midmorning we heard from the man who delivered our milk.

"Everyone's talking about it. They're scattered from the plaza all the way up the beach. You can barely see the sand. Disgusting! And everyone's down there checking it out—the mayor, the cops, the chamber of commerce. I don't know what's going to happen. I suppose they'll have to close the beach for a while. It kind of gives you the creeps, like an evil omen."

When the maid and I went down to see what was happening, we were met by a terrible stench at the shore road. Just as the milkman had said, everything had changed in the course of one night, as though the sea had brought a completely different beach to the shore.

The bathhouse, the ice cream stand, and the lifeguard station were all surrounded by a blanket of dead fish. The sea was gray and flat. The shining sun reflected off their scales.

Big ones, little ones, fat ones, thin ones, striped ones, mouths open, gills flayed. Some belly-up, some half buried in the sand, all piled one on top of the other, and all quite dead, with not so much as a twitch anywhere. There were certainly no open umbrellas on the beach today.

"Look, Mari," gasped the maid. "How do you think they got like that?" A crowd had gathered on the breakwater, and the TV station had sent a camera crew. People were taking pictures and discussing the strange sight; some had even gone down on the sand to examine the fish more closely. "This is terrible! All the tourists will leave town. What are we going to do? Your mother will be beside herself." But the maid seemed almost pleased. She grabbed my arm and pressed against me.

The spot where I had drunk my soda with the translator and his nephew the day before was buried under a drift of dead fish, and each wave brought more and more to the beach. Though the fish were dead, the mass of them seemed like some new living creature that had come from the bottom of the sea to attack us.

The tourists and locals could not stop discussing it, offering explanations: "Maybe somebody dumped them here out of spite." "No, it has to be some weird natural phenomenon." "It's been so hot, maybe even the fish couldn't stand it." "No, it's a curse, from a sailor who died at sea."

When the breeze blew in toward the shore, the smell was unbearable. Hands flew up to cover noses, and the maid buried her face in my shoulder. The stench was so foul it almost seemed my own brain was rotting; still, no one made a move to leave.

Over the next two days, a constant stream of trucks hauled the fish out of town. Experts appeared on television to explain that the unusual heat had raised the water temperature, causing a red tide. The fish had died from lack of oxygen. Some people insisted that the problem was toxic runoff from the paper plant. Everyone seemed uneasy, and the delivery people who came to the Iris reported the various theories that circulated through town. At any rate, no one wanted to eat fish for the time being.

Even after the trucks had taken away the last of it, there were still dead fish here and there around town. A car would run over one, squashing it flat. Then the liquefied organs would spill out and plaster it to the road. Careless souls who happened to step on these would leap back as if they had stumbled onto some omen of ill fortune.

"You're very good," I said, but he was apparently embarrassed and didn't look up.

"Not really. My uncle exaggerates." He had transferred his paintbrush to his left hand, freeing the right for the pendant. His wooden paint box was well used. It held a jumble of palettes, brushes, and tubes of paint, some of them new, and others squashed flat and nearly empty.

I was looking down at the beach from the bus stop when I'd spotted him. He was sitting on a rock at the edge of the water, painting a picture. I recognized him from the way he pushed back his hair, and from his pendant.

Descending the stairs on the breakwater, I came up behind the rock and called out to him. He seemed only mildly surprised to see me and simply nodded in my direction.

"I was waiting for guests at the bus stop, but they didn't come," I explained. He continued to work at his sketchbook. The picture, which seemed to be nearly finished, showed the sea and the ramparts, and the town beyond. He had also painted the island in the distance. "They phoned from the station to say they would be on the three thirty bus, but they must have missed it. I have nearly an hour until the next one." He did not answer me, but I didn't mind. I knew he understood me, and I was used to his silence. "How is your uncle?"

"He's busy with a rush job, translating an import permit for caviar." As he handed me the note, I realized that he had to stop painting in order to answer me, so I decided to sit quietly and watch for a while. I found a flat spot on the rock next to him in order to be out of the way. My feet were nearly dangling in the water.

The fish had been cleared away and the sea had returned to normal, but there were very few swimmers. The health department had tested the water and announced that it was safe, but their assurances had little effect. Most people were still upset by the fish and had no desire to swim. We'd had our share of cancellations at the Iris as well, and, just as the maid had predicted, Mother was in a foul mood. The heat had not broken, but with the departure of the tourists, the mood in town seemed more like autumn.

In his painting, the sea was a pale blue, dotted here and there with the white crests of waves. As his brush dabbed at the paper, the waves became more and more transparent. Though he seemed to pay little attention to fine details, he had captured the effect of the damp shells clinging to the seawall and the ear-shaped island protruding from the sea.

He squeezed dabs of color onto the palette, wet his brush in a cup of water, and mixed the paints until he had just the right shade. His eyes darted from his sketchbook to the palette to the scene before him. He also glanced over at me from time to time, but he never put down his brush to write me a note. From the uneven rock where we sat perched, everything—the paint box, the cup, and even the two of us—was at an angle.

"The spray will get you there. You should sit over here." He stopped painting at last and handed me this note. Then he moved his knapsack to make room next to him.

"Thanks," I said, sitting down where he had indicated.

"You don't have to go back to the hotel?"

"Mother will be angry if I don't wait for the guests. Do you mind if I stay here? I'll try not to bother you." He nodded and turned back to the sketchbook.

I began to wonder what the translator was doing. Was he flipping through a dictionary, looking up words with his magnifying glass? Writing down words about caviar in his careful characters? Had he put aside Marie's novel for the moment?

"What happened on the island the day the fish died?" I asked.

"Nothing out of the ordinary. Except that the coastline turned dark."

Depending on the direction of the wind, the fish smell still returned from time to time, as though the sand itself had taken on the stench of death.

A couple was sunbathing in deck chairs on the beach. A boy was windsurfing just offshore. A few children were gathering shells in the surf. Otherwise, the beach was empty. The drinks vendors and the lifeguards were gone. Hermit crabs cowered in the tidal pools on the rock where we were sitting, along with larger, bright red crabs and some sort of repulsive bug. The waves crashed again and again over the heavy silence of the beach.

"Why does your uncle live alone on the island?" When at last he put his brush in the cup of water, I asked the question that had been on my mind. "He has no telephone, no TV. No family or friends, no one comes to see him. . . . Except you."

"He has you." The sunlight on the white paper made the note hard to read. *"He's not the kind of man to have lots of friends. You're enough for him."*

"Has he told you about us?"

"No, but I can tell by looking at the two of you." He used a charcoal pencil to add shadows to the ramparts. As the paint

dried, the color of the sea had deepened. A crab tried to climb onto the paint box but lost its footing and fell into the water.

I wondered whether he really knew what went on between us. How could he know? My memories of what the translator had done seemed like nothing but beautiful illusions, even to me.

"He loves you," I said, but I immediately regretted speaking so openly. "I can feel it when I watch the two of you together. The way he looks at you with just a hint of worry in his eyes, the way he touches you whenever he can."

"He thinks of me as his son."

"No, it's not like that. Until you came, I would not have believed that he could give himself so completely to another person, the way he does with you."

I wanted to tell him that I ought to be the only one the translator wanted, that it was wrong of him to come between us. But I couldn't bring myself to say it.

"I remind him of his wife, who died too young." The characters flowed from his pen like a long, thin design, and though he had painted and written a great deal, he never seemed to tire. *"He dotes on me as a kind of penance."*

"Penance for what?"

"Not for anything he did. There's really no one to blame. In the end, it was just a terrible accident."

"But how did she die?"

"She caught her scarf in a train door." I read the note three times, unable to grasp the meaning of the words. *"My uncle*

had been invited by a Russian university and he was leaving for
Moscow. The train hadn't arrived yet. I was just a baby, and my
aunt was holding me on the platform. My uncle was about to take
our picture when the train we were standing beside began to move.
No one realized that her scarf was caught in the door."

"But what happened?" The tip of his pen ran across the
paper, the sound lost in the waves. He coughed, bit a fingernail, tapped the toe of his tennis shoe on the rock. I could hear
the noises he made more clearly than I could have heard any
words. Eventually, his hand reached out to deliver the next
note, and for that one moment, the tips of our fingers met. His
were covered with paint.

"They finally realized what was happening when the train be-
gan dragging her along the platform, but there was nothing they
could do. My mother screamed. My aunt was being strangled and
pulled away more and more quickly—and I was still in her arms.
In the end, her head hit the last pillar on the platform and she died
instantly. Her skull was crushed, her neck was broken, and the scarf
had burned away all the skin on her neck. But she still had me tight
in her arms, and there wasn't a scratch on me."

He had written all of this hunched over his notepad,
scribbling intently, without once stopping or hesitating, as if
he had the whole story memorized from constant repetition.
Even words like "crushed" and "burned" didn't seem so terrible in his graceful blue characters.

"Of course, I don't remember any of this," he added. *"My mother*
told me everything."

"And there was nothing your uncle could have done?"

"*Nothing. He just called after her to drop the baby so she could untie the scarf. I don't know what would have happened to me if she had listened to him. But it's pointless to wonder about that. At any rate, there were bad feelings between my mother and my uncle after that—I suppose because he'd been willing to sacrifice me to save his wife.*"

The scene came to me in these tiny scraps of paper—the dim light of the platform, the large, pale face of the clock, flashbulbs, high-heeled shoes clattering across the concrete, unbearable pain, the cold metal of the pillar.

"*I have no way of knowing whether my mother's memories are accurate. I suppose no one's to blame. But one thing's certain: we were all badly damaged by that little breeze that tugged at the end of her scarf. . . .*"

"I've seen the scarf," I said. "He keeps it hidden in a drawer."

"*I suppose it's a souvenir of sorts, even though it took his wife from him. Eventually, he disappeared, and by the time I heard the story, no one knew where to find him. But we met up again by chance the year I entered university. He seemed delighted to have found me, and he spoiled me rather shamelessly. Even though, as you've seen from my story, he had been willing for me to die that day long ago.*"

"Are the stories he tells about you as a child true?"

"*I told him all those stories; he exaggerates a bit. It's another form of penance, I suppose—to erase that one moment in the past. He knows it's pointless, but he can't help himself. As soon as he sees me,*" *he falls back into the pattern . . . sometimes grateful that I can't talk."*

He had written so much I began to worry that he would run out of paper. My worrying grew almost uncontrollable— there was still so much more I wanted to know about the translator, if only his nephew could go on handing me notes forever.

The setting sun illuminated his profile. His lips remained tightly sealed. The chain around his neck glistened with sweat.

It suddenly occurred to me that he would be old one day, just like the translator. I tried to picture him with wrinkled skin, slack muscles, and thinning hair, but no image came to me. No matter how carefully I studied him, I could not find the shadow of age on his body.

I looked at my watch. The bus would arrive in less than ten minutes.

"When are you leaving?" I asked.

"Tomorrow."

"Tomorrow? Your uncle will be sad to see you go."

"No, he'll be happy to get back to his normal routine."

"And will you come back next summer?"

"I'm not sure when I'll be back. I'm going to study in Italy this fall." He touched the paper to be sure the paint had dried and then closed his sketchbook. He put away his brushes in

the paint box and tipped the cup of water into the sea. The waves carried away the cloud of colors.

"Does it seem strange to you?" I asked. He stopped for a moment and turned to me with a questioning look. "The fifty-year difference in our ages. You couldn't call it normal."

"It doesn't seem strange to me. I'm happy for both of you. And I'm happy I got to meet you." I didn't know how to respond, so I helped him replace the caps on the tubes of paint. *"I've been coming to this town for years now, but you're the first person I've ever spoken to other than my uncle."*

"But I worry sometimes. We have no future together, and I'm afraid everything will end with summer."

"Everything will work out," he wrote. *"Don't be afraid of breezes and scarves."* He pressed this last note into my hand, which was overflowing now with his words. We started to stand up, but our footing on the rock was unsteady and we nearly fell into the sea. Then, suddenly, we were embracing. I'm not sure whether I stumbled and he reached out to steady me, or whether we were embracing even before I lost my balance. I felt as though the waves had stopped.

We kissed. Our lips met without hesitation, as though we had each decided long ago that it would happen. My hand still clutched the sheaf of notes. The pendant dangled against my chest, a cool thing between our warm bodies.

When I asked him to come with me to the Iris, he couldn't answer; his pendant was trapped between us. But he blended in with the two groups of guests I met at the bus stop and followed me up to the hotel. It was an adventure. He played the part of a mute young man on a trip to do some sketching. I put one of the groups in 204 and the other in 305. Then I gave him the key to 202—the room the translator and the prostitute had used. In the register it had been stamped with the red cancellation mark.

Some children were running around the lobby, ignoring their parents' attempts to calm them down. Another group of guests had spread out a map on the front desk to look for a restaurant. He took advantage of the confusion to slip up to the room.

The light was dim in Room 202, the windows clouded with steam from the processing plant next door. The sound of the machine that mixed the fish paste was barely audible. The beds were made up. The Bible and the telephone were on the night table, a box of tissues had been set in front of the mirror, a corkscrew and a chipped glass were arranged on top of the refrigerator—everything in its appointed place. But the people who were supposed to stay here tonight had called to cancel this morning.

He was in no hurry. Nor was he made anxious by the sound of voices in the hallway or footsteps on the stairs. He took his time as he touched me. The sketchbook and paint box lay abandoned under the bed.

He did not tie me up; he did not hit me. Nor did he give me a single command. I did have trouble breathing, as I had with the translator, but this time it was from the weight of his broad chest pressing down on mine. His fingers ran over my body as skillfully as they scrawled the characters in his notes. His hip bones were hard against my thighs.

The bed groaned so loudly I worried that they would be able to hear it downstairs. Someone was gargling in the room above us. The bell on the front desk rang. The warmth of his body filled me.

He let out a muffled cry, and I knew it was over. I was certain it was his voice. The faintest cry, lodged deep in his chest, suddenly escaped through his parted lips.

"Would you show me your tongue?" I asked. He climbed back into the T-shirt and pants he had discarded on the other bed, and then he put his pendant back around his neck.

"Why?"

"I don't know."

He took hold of my shoulders and then cautiously opened his mouth. It was dark inside—no tongue, just a black cavity. The darkness was so deep that I felt dizzy staring down into it.

Just at that moment, there was an irritated cry from the lobby.

"Mari! Mari! Where are you?" It was Mother. Footsteps came running up the stairs and then down the hall toward our room. In an instant, I had grabbed the sketchbook and paint box and pushed him ahead of me into the closet. The box clattered against the wall. My body stiffened and I clung to him. Mother knocked on the door of Room 201.

"I've come to change the quilts," she called. Her voice

seemed to be right outside the closet. I pushed even closer, and he wrapped his arm around me. "Housekeeping!" Mother called out, this time taking the master key from the pocket of her apron and fitting it in the door of 202.

My heart was pounding and my chest contracted, exactly as it had the day I skipped school and hid in Room 301. The same pain as when the translator strangled me with the scarf. The smell of varnish in the closet stung my eyes.

Mother walked around the room, passing in front of the closet to check the lock on the window. Then she drew back the curtains. I couldn't keep from peeking through the crack in the closet door, even though I had the feeling I would be safer if I shut my eyes. The vibrations from Mother's swollen feet came to me through the floor. I was terrified by everything—by Mother, and by the nephew and the things he had done to me, but especially by the thought that the translator knew nothing of all this.

Mother's fingers brushed the nightstand where he had set his pendant, checking for dust. Then she straightened the cover on the bed where we had been a moment before. I was afraid that she would feel the lingering heat from our bodies, or that she would find a hair—she would know it was mine.

Our hearts were beating together, and my ear was damp from his breath. His hair smelled of the sea. Mother looked around the room once more, frowned disapprovingly, and then closed the door behind her. I could hear her steps retreating down the hall.

The strength drained from my body and I slipped from his arms, collapsing to the closet floor. The sliver of light from the crack in the door only made it seem darker, and when I looked up, I could barely see him. He seemed to retreat further into the shadows each time I blinked.

After we crawled out of the closet, we had been so worried Mother would find us that he immediately slipped out the back and ran off. The next day, I'd thought he might stop at the Iris before leaving town, but he never came. The only people who appeared in the lobby that afternoon were an elderly couple who had called to reserve three months in advance and a man selling dustcloths. At some point I realized that the last bus had left town, and I would never have any more notes to add to the ones in my pocket. But now I had the translator to myself again.

A strange quiet had descended on the town. The beach was nearly empty except for the gulls, and even at noon there were plenty of seats on the restaurant terraces. Everyone seemed idle, from the ticket sellers at the seawall and the rental boat piers to the women at the snow cone stands, even the taxi drivers. Though it was still midseason, some of the souvenir shops had already decided to close. On sunny days, the light on the deserted shore road seemed even brighter than usual.

That day, however, it was overcast for the first time in weeks. Midday was no lighter than dawn. Layers of steel blue clouds obscured the sun—the same color as the sea. It was an ominous color. Not beautiful but somehow pure, like the steady pulse of calm breathing. A narrow strip of sky showed at the horizon, but the clouds seemed to weigh down on it, threatening to crush it at any moment. A gull looked up from a rock, as if hesitant to fly.

We were standing on the deck of the excursion boat, looking out at the sea. The crowd that had pressed against the railing until so recently was nowhere to be seen. A nurse from the sanitarium who had apparently been shopping in town was sleeping against the window in the cabin. The man who ran the coffee stand had left his post and was smoking a cigarette at the bow of the boat. The deck was empty except for a few groups of tourists out to escape the monotony of town.

"So he's gone home?" I asked, though I knew the answer.

"Yes," the translator said. For some reason, it seemed strange to receive an immediate answer to a question without a moment of silence for the opening of the note case, the ripping of the paper, the scrawl of the pen. I was still in the rhythm of conversation with his nephew.

"The week seemed so short," I said.

"He can never stay long. He doesn't want his mother to know he comes here."

"Why is that?"

"Most children that age have secrets from their mothers."

"Everyone who comes to your house has secrets."

"That's true," he said, turning to me with a thin smile. "Perhaps the island would sink if they were ever revealed."

The boat's engine vibrated under our feet. The wind was stronger than usual, and our skin was damp. My hair was still pinned up, but some wisps hung down on my forehead. He had reached out several times to brush them back, but it was useless as long as the wind was blowing.

"When will he visit you again?"

"I'm not sure. I never know until the last minute when he's coming."

I wasn't sure whether he knew that his nephew was going to study in Italy, but I decided not to mention it. I didn't want to tell him what had happened at the Iris, so it seemed best not to mention our encounter on the rocks or anything else about that day.

The translator was wearing the same brown suit with wide lapels he had worn the day we went to the circus. I remembered seeing the paisley necktie when I had searched the wardrobe. He washed the ice cream stain from his pants.

"What strange weather!" I said. Threatening clouds loomed low over the boat. There was a breeze, but the sea was calm. There was no sign of the sailboats or fishing trawlers that would normally have ventured offshore. "Do you think it will finally rain?"

"Yes, it could be quite a storm," he said.

"We haven't had rain in over a month. I've almost forgotten what it looks like." I leaned against the rail and stared at the horizon, trying to guess where the rain would start. But there was no rain, just a blue veil that covered the sea, the translator's face, and my hands in front of me. The clouds seemed to be bearing down, swallowing everything around us.

"Don't worry," he said, wrapping his arm around my back. "You'll remember right away." He was clumsy and hesitant at times like this, as though even the slightest contact with my body was somehow momentous and complex. Which struck me as strange, so different from his nephew's self-assured kiss on the rocks. And yet the translator had seen me in the most shameful positions.

I turned to look back at the shore, but the town was no longer in view, and the tide had covered the seawall. The gull that had been hesitating on the rail finally opened its wings and flew away, vanishing almost immediately into the low clouds. The vortex from the boat's propeller sucked up flotsam from the sea—driftwood, seaweed, empty cans, bits of Styrofoam, fishing line, plastic bags. . . .

The nurse who had been sleeping in the lounge woke for a moment, rubbed her hand on the window, and peered out at the weather. But she went right back to sleep. The windowsill had left a red mark on half her face. A middle-aged couple with a video camera walked past. They paused in front of the man from the coffee stand, who was sitting on a bench on deck.

"How long do we stop at the island?" the wife asked. "I'd like to have a look around." I couldn't hear the man's answer, perhaps because he was facing into the wind. After the couple moved on, he lit another cigarette. He looked over at us from time to time, but when I met his glance he looked quickly away and puffed at his cigarette.

As the boat turned slowly to the left, its foghorn echoed in the distance. Between the clouds and the sea, the island appeared.

I sat on the couch and watched the translator work. Sitting bolt upright at his desk, he traced a line of Russian characters with his left hand while his right wrote down the translation in his notebook. From time to time he would pause to flip through a dictionary, or fiddle with his reading glasses, or stare thoughtfully into space.

He had been asked to translate a letter that had come from Russia to the neurosurgery department at a university hospital. He pulled a medical dictionary from the very bottom of his bookshelf, explaining that the project was particularly difficult because of the technical terminology. Marie's novel had been put away in a drawer.

He had shown me his books with obvious pride. "You have a dictionary for everything, don't you?" I said.

"Indeed I do. Philosophy, logic, mechanics, music, art, computers, cinema . . . one for every field of human endeavor." The dictionaries were thick and impressive but badly worn, the titles on their spines almost illegible and the bindings tattered. Each time he turned a page of the medical dictionary, there was an odd ripping sound, as if the whole volume were about to come apart. But the translator handled the books tenderly, reminding me of the way he had unfastened my blouse button by button, or how his fingers had searched between my legs for the tender spot.

I sipped the tea he had made for me. It was delicious, and the pot was full. The wind had been blowing harder since the boat docked, and the branches of the pine trees that lined the bluff above the cove were nodding to the west. The windows rattled continually, and during one particularly strong gust, I wondered whether the house might be blown away.

It was not raining, but the clouds covered the whole sky now, all the way to the horizon. Their blue light reached deep into the room, even through the drawn curtains.

"Is it difficult?" I asked quietly, having waited for a moment when the wind was less deafening. He did not turn to look at me, and his pen continued to move over the page. "Do you take notes first and then write out a clean copy? . . . Do you have much more to do?" He turned and put his finger to his lips to silence me. Then he went back to his work. I said nothing more.

The room had reverted to its original state after the departure of his nephew. The house was once again filled with foreboding—no more radio, cheerful meals, or hibiscus.

I tried to remember how the nephew had looked sitting on this very couch, but I could not. The touch of his lips on the rock and even the single word he had uttered on the bed at the Iris seemed like something from the distant past, long before I had met the translator. Now my mind was filled with memories of a cord, pain running through my body, stern commands. Even the rhythm of the conversations with the nephew that I had found so intimate, even that had been blown away with the wind.

The translator underlined a sentence in the letter. His finger hovered over a spot in the dictionary. He coughed, sat up straighter, and then continued writing, paying careful attention to each character.

I had to be patient until he finished translating the letter. But I knew that soon he would be paying such careful attention to me. Only with me did his old, withered body come to life. The fingers clutching the pen would grasp my breast, the lips pursed in thought would probe between my ribs, the feet hidden under the desk would trample my face.

I took a sip of tea without taking my eyes off him. The boards of the terrace creaked. The wind pushed an empty flowerpot across the lawn. But the surface of the sea was as smooth and flat as ever.

What would he say when he finally turned to look at me? That was my only concern at the moment. Would he call me a filthy sow? Or tell me to lick the floor? Or to spread my legs?

He took hundreds of pictures. He set the flash, adjusted the lens, changed the roll of film. I had no idea he was so skilled with a camera. For my part, I assumed every imaginable pose—amazed at the number of shapes a human body could take. He needed more cord than usual to create all of these positions, but he had bought extra for the occasion.

First, he undressed me. That was always the most important thing. When, at the very end, he stripped away my underpants, I could see how ugly I was.

Then he tied me to a chair—the one he had been working in a moment earlier. It was a sturdy wooden chair with a leather seat. He pulled my arms behind my back and bound my wrists, then ran the cord again and again around my ribs. Now I would have to carry the chair with me everywhere I went. It was heavy, and I teetered under the weight. When I lost my balance, the cord cut into my breasts. I groaned, but he paid no attention and ordered me to lock the kitchen door, to clear away the teacups, to remove the quilt from the bed.

"You do all this at the Iris, you must be used to it."

The chair on my back knocked into the walls and furniture, tightening the knots. I used every part of my body that remained free, my chin and mouth, my sides and legs, to turn the lock, carry the cups, fold the quilt. He followed me around, snapping pictures the whole time. My face contorted with pain, my breasts dripping with spilled tea, my body staggering through the bedroom.

When I finished my chores, he bound my feet to the legs of the chair so I couldn't move at all. My joints were bent at unnatural angles, and my hands and feet were numb and cold. I felt as though I had become a chair, my skin the leather, my fat the cushion, my bones the wood. A chair from the tips of my fingers to the tips of my toes.

The translator sat down in the chair. He smiled happily, rested his elbows on the arms, crossed his legs. My body supported his whole weight.

"Heavy?" he asked, looking back at me. I couldn't answer, not even a nod. "What a comfortable chair," he said, slowly stroking the armrests and the back. I had no idea whether he was rubbing the chair or me.

I became other things as well. A table, a shoe cupboard, a clock, a sink, a garbage can. He used the cord to twist my body into these shapes, tying my arms and legs, my hips, my chest, my neck. He worked quickly, binding wrists to drawer pulls, hips to doors, fingers to knobs. The cord obeyed him, and he used it to bend and tie me into whatever shape was in his head.

My whole body was red with rope burns. The skin wasn't broken, but there was a great deal of pain. It spread across my skin, and as it dissolved into a single, sharp agony, I was overcome with pleasure. I went happily to fetch his shoes in the hall. In the bathroom, I gratefully received the saliva he spat into my mouth.

When he opened the door at the back of the kitchen, I had no idea what was waiting for me. I found myself in a small, dark, windowless room. All four walls were lined to the ceiling with shelves. The air was stale and dry, with a powdery smell of soap and flour and dust.

It was the pantry. The shelves were stocked with food of all sorts, and what didn't fit had been piled on the floor: canned goods, rice, spaghetti, chocolate, mineral water, wine. . . . I wondered how many years it would take him to eat all of this by himself. The shelves sagged under the weight of his provisions and seemed on the verge of collapsing.

"Go on," he said, his voice filling the little room. Once we were both inside, there was no space. He took down a bunch of onions suspended from a hook on the ceiling. The onions looked delicious, with pale, papery skin.

"Get down on the floor," he said. The orders came one after the other. He passed a chain through the cord binding my wrists and pulled it up on the hook. Suddenly, he seemed extraordinarily strong. He had no idea how to swim and could not even properly hold an ice cream cone, but he could hang a body from the ceiling with total ease.

The flashbulbs blinded me. The wind seemed more remote now, but it continued to howl. The rattling of the doors and windows reached deep into the pantry. The lens came peering in at the bulging muscles on my neck, my exposed sex, the sweaty backs of my legs. I could not see his face behind the camera, but I could tell from the way he grasped it with his fingers that his contempt for me was absolute. My body revolved imperceptibly in space. The chain grated against the hook, making a noise that only heightened the pain.

Suspended above the floor, I suddenly knew I could no longer escape. My wrists seemed about to rip from my arms, and I pictured the scene to myself. My skin would peel away, the flesh would tear, and finally the chain would break the bones. I would fall to the floor with a sharp snap, then hold my arms in front of my eyes, only to discover that there was nothing left below the wrists. Thick drops fall from above, and when I look up, the head of the translator's wife is hanging from the hook—with the scarf still wrapped around her neck.

His back was illuminated by the thin strip of light coming from the kitchen. I could sense moisture in the wind—perhaps the rain had started at last.

He changed the film again, pulling roll after roll from the pocket of his jacket. Suddenly, there was a sound of movement in a corner. The translator kicked aside a bag of rice to reveal a small cage trap. Inside was a young mouse.

"Poor thing," he said. The mouse's tail was caught, and it squealed and dragged the cage behind it, trying to escape. "It has to be punished."

The struggling and writhing must have caused the mouse great pain. If the tail ripped from the body, it would certainly bleed. What color was mouse blood?

The translator pulled a riding crop from between two jars. I hadn't noticed it concealed on the dark shelves.

It was long and flexible. The velvet handle glistened with

sweat. It must have been much like the one that Marie's beloved riding master had carried. He brought it down against my thigh and then flicked it back in a lovely arc through the air—so lovely I almost forgot that it was meant to hurt me. He changed the angle ever so slightly with each stroke, so it never left the same mark twice. He whipped my flesh in the crowded pantry, never striking the shelves or the wall or the chain, but always finding me.

More than the pain, it was the sound that captivated me. It was high and pure, like a stringed instrument. The whip played these notes on my body, contracting the organs or bones concealed beneath the skin. I would never have believed that I could make such fascinating sounds, as though the whip were releasing wells of music from the deepest cavities in my body.

The mouse was still trying to escape, but the more it struggled, the tighter the trap held its tail. It was slumped over on its side now, its eyes dark and damp. It ground its tiny teeth and squealed incessantly.

The whip snapped again, sending pain from my shoulder down my side. I cried in ecstasy, drowning out the squeaking of the mouse.

THIRTEEN

The storm had broken over the island by the time we emerged from the pantry. Rain beat against the windows, the wind swirled, and the surf washed deep into the cove. Waves crashed on the rocks below, shooting white spray in the dark. The roar of the sea and the howling of the wind shook the whole island. The translator turned on the light in the room.

The mouse was dead, drowned in a bucket of water. It floated on the surface, curled in a ball. The front legs were limp and its mouth half open. When the translator had picked it up by the tail and plunged it in the water, it had thrashed about for a moment. But it had stopped very quickly and lay still with its eyes wide open, as though considering some important problem. It had not suffered terribly. When he let go of the tail, it had bobbed to the surface.

I looked at the translator, and he was staring at the floor

where he had thrown my skirt. He walked over, picked it up, reached in the pocket, and in his hand he held the slips of paper.

"Did you see him in town?" he asked. I flinched. "Did you meet?" I realized he was talking about his nephew.

"Yes," I said, unable to keep from looking at them. The pages were wrinkled from my pocket.

"When?"

"The day before he left."

"He didn't tell me. . . ."

"I just happened to see him painting on the rocks near the bus stop."

"I didn't know you'd met without me."

"It was only for a few minutes."

"Yet he wrote all these notes?" He frowned and thought for a moment, as he always did when digesting some news. The notes slipped one by one from his hand. I glimpsed the nephew's familiar handwriting, but I couldn't remember clearly what he had written.

"I'm sure he didn't think it was worth mentioning. We just chatted for a moment while he was drawing and I was waiting for the bus. That's all."

"He wrote about my wife. About her death."

"I asked him to tell me."

"But why didn't you mention it?"

"I didn't think it was important."

"There's only one reason to have kept it secret—you didn't want me to know what happened between the two of you."

"But he's gone. And nothing happened!"

"Liar!" I'd heard this tone countless times since that first night at the Iris. It always paralyzed me. A violent gust of wind swept across the island, and we could hear something splintering and blown away, a pine tree on the cliff or the rail on the deck. "I can see it in his handwriting. He wrote all this as you talked, and I can tell how he felt, what you were doing, I can almost hear it."

The wind and the rain swirled together outside the window. The last note fell from his hand.

"I betrayed you," I said, so quietly that I hardly knew it was my own voice. It felt like a lie even though I told the truth. He stood perfectly still. A siren sounded, long and low.

"You can't get home. They've stopped the boat," he said.

Strangely, I did not think about Mother, or what I would tell her tomorrow. It seemed that tomorrow would never come, that the storm would never stop and we would be trapped on the island forever. This thought made me all the more excited.

The translator devised a punishment for me, a superb penalty that would never have occurred to anyone else. He dragged me into the bathroom and cut off my hair.

It was terribly cold. The ventilator fan whirred. Though the room itself was small, the ceiling was very high and the sound of the scissors echoed overhead. Several tiles had come off the walls and floor, and the bathtub was badly cracked.

"What did you do?" he said, brandishing the scissors he had once used to cut away my slip. As he had done that day, he snapped them above me again and again. The sound rang in my ears.

I didn't know what sort of damage the scissors could do to my body, but I remembered that my slip had fallen to pieces at the slightest touch, and with no effort at all he had rendered me naked.

"How could you have seduced someone so dear to me?" Somehow my hair had retained much of its shape until that moment; then he grabbed it and let it fall in front of my face. "I'm going to teach you a lesson. Just like this!" He grabbed it again and pulled my head in circles.

"Stop," I screamed, kicking the sink and falling against the tub. I felt as though my scalp would tear from my skull. "Please stop! You're hurting me!" The cold blades touched my head, and the knot of hair he had gathered in his hand fell to the floor. The camellia oil had evaporated, and the hair was stiff and dry. The scissors slashed over my head again and again, and long after I thought there could be nothing left, he kept on, unwilling to forgive me.

"I'm sorry," I said, again and again. "It's over!" But he paid no attention. I wanted him to punish me. Perhaps that was why I had invited the boy to the Iris in the first place.

There was hair everywhere, on my lips, my breasts, my sex. I tried to brush it off, but it clung fast. It covered his hands, and his normally immaculate suit. Outside the window, it was pitch black. Raindrops slithered down the pane.

The scissors fell from his fingers and clattered on the tile. He bent over, coughing and gasping for breath. Then we stood frozen for a long time. I wanted to reach up to feel my head, but my hand was trembling.

He turned the knob on the shower, releasing a cascade of hot water. Hair swirled toward the drain, eddying around the edges of the tiles and the soap dish, as if it were reluctant to go. I found it hard to believe that this tangle of thin black hair had been on my head like some parasite just a moment ago. The strands twisted and squirmed, trying to find an escape, but in the end they all went resolutely down the drain.

Then he turned the shower on me. I retreated into the corner and tried to cover my face, but he came after me with the nozzle. The stream of water was so powerful, I could barely open my eyes and mouth. It flooded my nose and ears and made it hard to breathe.

"How's that?" he asked, turning the knob again. "Shall we make it hotter?" A snarl of hair blocked the drain. I couldn't breathe—I was drowning.

Later that night, the electricity failed. Without light, the wind seemed even closer. The rain showed no sign of ending. The translator changed out of his wet clothes, but it was too dark to tell which suit and tie he had chosen. I was still naked.

He set out candles, one each on his desk and the coffee table and the dining table. Then made dinner—something orange and soupy. Ladling it into a shallow bowl, he set it on the floor, and I got down on my hands and knees to lap it up. I was clumsy, and the liquid spilled from the corners of my mouth, staining my neck orange. He said nothing—ate nothing, drank nothing—but just sat on the couch watching me.

I looked over at the bookcase as discreetly as I could, studying my reflection in the glass. My head, floating there in the pale, milky light, was both pathetic and laughable—like a chick with bedraggled feathers. The hair was a tangled mess, hacked unevenly across my scalp, shooting out at all angles. I blinked to be sure I was looking at my own reflection. I licked my lips, and the ruffled chick licked hers.

"Eat!" he said. The candles flickered. Mother would no longer be able to gather my hair in a bun, or smooth it with camellia oil. Stray clippings rained down on the dish, making delicate patterns in the orange pool. I lapped them up on my tongue.

The long night wore on. It seemed like an age ago that I had stood on the deck of the boat and looked out at the clouds. Everything outside the house had been blown away by the storm—the sea, the town, the flower clock, even the Iris.

He had inflicted every sort of misery and humiliation on me, and every sort of pleasure, there in the pale light of the candles. The mouse was the only witness, floating in the bucket.

We were the only passengers on the first boat in the morning. The storm had passed, but the sea was still rough.

Rays of sunlight found their way through breaks in the clouds.

I had tied a scarf—the one that had strangled his wife—over my head. The translator's handkerchiefs were all too small and the towels in the bathroom too ugly. There was nothing else in the house.

I had told him it didn't matter, that I could go as I was, but he had brought me the scarf. When I hesitated, he wrapped it around my head. He hid the frayed edge behind my neck, and from a distance the bloodstains seemed to be part of the pattern.

"It looks wonderful on you," he said.

The deck was wet, so we held hands to keep from slipping. The marks on my wrists were faintly visible. The cocoa he bought me at the coffee stand was lukewarm and very sweet. Behind the stand was the same man who had been smoking at the bow the day before. He seemed surly, and his puffy eyes never looked up as the translator handed him the money. Only when I thanked him did he glance up, his eyes lingering on the scarf.

The sea was gray and dotted with bits of garbage that had washed out from the river. Clouds streamed across the sky, but there were no shorebirds in sight.

"The rail is wet," he said, wiping it with his handkerchief.

"What should I tell Mother?"

"Tell her you went out to the island and couldn't get back. That's the truth, isn't it? Just say they let you stay the night at the sanatarium."

"But what will I tell her about my hair?"

"Leave the scarf on. It's lovely, and I'm sure your mother will like it."

I put my hand to my head. The material was stiff where the bloodstains remained. A gust of wind tugged at the scarf, and the translator reached out to tie the knot more tightly.

The town was coming into view. First the church steeple and the tower on the town hall, and then the seawall, which seemed to float above the sea. The boat slowed and blew its horn, making a lazy turn to the right. I squeezed his hand. The man at the coffee stand was washing my cocoa cup.

We could see a crowd gathered on the pier, as though the tourists had been waiting all this time for the boat to arrive. We made a quarter-turn and approached from the stern, the horn blowing a deeper note this time.

"We can say good-bye here," I said.

"No, I'll see you as far as the clock."

"But I've got to run home. The guests will be checking out."

"I'll write you then."

"I'll be waiting." He touched my cheek and then closed his hand carefully, as if to preserve the sensation. There was a buzzing in the distance, and I thought I heard someone calling my name.

"Mari! Mari!" The people on the dock were looking up at us, and they were not tourists. There was a waiter in an apron, a taxi driver, a middle-aged woman in her bathrobe—

all whispering to one another. A police car and an ambulance were parked in front of the waiting room. I recognized the young musician from the plaza at the back of the crowd. His accordion was around his neck as usual, but he was not playing.

"Mari! I'm here! Mari!"

It was Mother. She was screaming from the dock. But why was she calling my name over and over? It struck me as very strange.

The engine rattled to a stop. Two young men came running up on deck and shouted something at us. They were yelling, but I couldn't understand a word. One would shout a few words, and then the other, but in my ears there was nothing but silence. No sound reached me, as though my eardrums had suddenly evaporated.

The translator let go of my hand and stumbled away, fleeing across the deck. One of the men ran after him while the other came and put his arms around me. He was still talking, but I heard nothing.

The translator tripped over an ashtray. The man from the coffee stand caught him, pinning his arms in back, but he managed to shake free and ran toward the bow of the boat. The scene played out in silence.

Just as they were about to catch him, he leapt into the sea. Without a word of farewell or even a smile in my direction, he threw his leg over the rail, curled in a ball, and fell. There was a splash, and at that instant my hearing returned.

"Are you hurt?" The young man peered into my eyes. His tone was gentle.

"He jumped! Lower a lifeboat." Footsteps running across the deck. A clamor of voices. "Get a life preserver!"

The young man tried to touch the scarf, but I brushed his hand away and crouched down on the deck.

"Mari! You must have been terrified! But you're safe now. I nearly died when they told me you'd been kidnapped. And look what he's done to you. You're not hurt anywhere? What a monster! But I'm glad you're all right. That's the most important thing. And thank you, Officer. You'll be taking her to the hospital? In an ambulance?" Mother rambled on, her voice slipping around and around me, tighter and tighter, but it was the sound of the translator sinking into the sea that echoed in my ears.

His body surfaced three days later. The police diving team found it, swollen and half naked. The head had ballooned to twice its normal size, and the face was almost unrecognizable.

I learned he'd had a criminal record. More than four years ago, he had attacked the owner of a clock shop in a dispute about some purchase. He had beaten the man with one of his clocks. Now, his fingerprint record from that old arrest had made it possible to identify his body when it washed ashore.

I spent only one night in the hospital. The doctors examined every inch of me, checking each little bruise and scrape and recording it on my chart. They discovered that my head was covered with countless tiny cuts that must have been from the blades of the scissors. They stung when I rubbed against the pillow.

The police inquiry was careful but discreet. It was conducted by a female detective, who was sometimes accompanied by a psychiatrist or a counselor. But I simply told them that I had no memory of anything that had happened. They assumed this was the result of the shock, and they concluded that, since the suspect was dead, there was little point in pursuing an inquiry that could have little benefit for the victim and was likely to prolong her suffering.

There had been a tremendous uproar at the Iris when I didn't return on the night of the storm, and my absence had been reported to the police. At first they'd assumed I had been carried away by a wave or drowned in a flash flood. But in the morning, the waiter from the coffee stand on the boat said that he'd seen me with a suspicious-looking man. I learned the details from the maid. She talked breathlessly, unable to contain her curiosity but realizing she had to appear sympathetic at the same time.

But none of it meant anything to me. The translator was dead. That was my only reality.

I didn't return to my duties behind the front desk, preferring to avoid the eyes of the guests. It took more than ten months for my hair to grow back. But even when it did, Mother no longer insisted on putting it up for me. Eventually, the camellia oil dried in the bottle.

No one came to claim the translator's body, and it was cremated and placed in the public grave. The nephew was never seen in town again.

I did ask the police to look for the translation of the novel about Marie, but they were never able to locate it. All they found were endless rolls of film filled with pictures of me.

Since 1988, Yoko Ogawa has written more than twenty works of fiction and non-fiction, and has won every major Japanese literary award. Her fiction has appeared in the *New Yorker*, *A Public Space*, and *Zoetrope*. Harvill Secker published *The Diving Pool*, a collection of three novellas, in 2007 and her novel *The Housekeeper and the Professor* in 2009.